Amy Cross is the author of more than 100 horror, paranormal, fantasy and thriller novels.

THE
OTHER ANN

AMY CROSS

This edition
first published by Dark Season Books,
United Kingdom, 2019

ISBN: 9781081831752

Also available in e-book format.

www.amycross.com

AMY CROSS

CONTENTS

THE OTHER ANN

AMY CROSS

PROLOGUE

I HATE EVERYONE.

Storming down the path that leads from our house, I realize after a moment that I'm clenching my fists. Thirty seconds ago, I came *this* close to punching my stupid cousin Ian. Just because he's eleven, just because he's one year old than me, he thinks he can boss me around. And everyone just laughs, as if it's the funniest thing in the world ever.

Stopping once I'm past the trees, I sit down and roll my right sleeve up. When Ian grabbed me, he left a really big red mark, and I think I'm going to get a bruise soon. I poke the area, and then I gasp as I feel a burst of soreness.

Hearing voices shouting in the distance, I turn and look back toward the house. Counting all the aunts, uncles and cousins who have come to visit this weekend, there are twenty people in our house right now, filling it so much that I feel as if the walls are about to fall down. The noise is horrible, and there's not even anywhere to hide away. There are people in every room, even in *my* room, which I'm having to share with three of my cousins.

I hate people. When I grow up, I don't want to ever see anyone ever again. I want to live alone forever. I don't need anyone else around me.

All I need is myself.

CHAPTER ONE

Twenty years later...

THIS IS PERFECT.

As I sit at my desk, I hear the coffee machine whirring to life. A fresh cappuccino will be ready in precisely two and a half minutes. While I wait, I sit back and stare at the latest sketch, the one that I completed late last night. I've been working on the design of a three-bed lake house for a client on the other side of the country. When I went to bed, I thought the design was complete, but now I'm wondering whether I could do something more interesting with the garage area. I'm ahead of schedule on the assignment, so I can afford to take another day or two to mull things over.

After a moment, I realize I can hear a distant

buzzing sound.

I turn and look out the window. At first, I see only the gravel driveway that leads off between the trees. Still, the buzzing sound is getting louder, and I know exactly what it means. Getting to my feet, I step away from the desk and head toward the front door. As I go, the television on the far wall flickers to life. I have it set to switch on at precisely 7am, with the aim being to force myself to watch the news for a few minutes. As much as I hate the rest of the world, I suppose I should keep track of developments, just in case some unaccountable idiot somewhere has pushed us to the verge of some fresh disaster.

The front door slides open and I step out onto the porch, just as the postal drone flies into view. It's been six months now since I signed up for this experimental form of delivery, and I can't help smiling as I see the drone bringing its little load containing my weekly mail. Before the drone, I had that obnoxious mailman coming to the house once a week. No matter how hard I tried to get him to just leave the mail on the porch, he always wanted to try striking up a conversation. Now that the drone is up and running, I never have to see another human being. In fact, it has now been exactly one month since I had to see anyone face-to-face. I call that a victory.

The drone reaches the porch and then drops

down, and two sets of mechanical pincers begin to open. A couple of letters drop onto the wooden decking, and then the drone rises back up. I smile at the round, dark camera on its tip.

"Hey," I say. "Nice day."

Ignoring me, the drone turns and starts buzzing off back toward the gravel path. It's a cute little machine, and I quite like the thought of it zooming away through the forest, heading back to the delivery office several miles away. As I reach down and pick up my mail, I can't help feeling that the drone has been a godsend. Sure, this service is expensive, but any price is worth paying if it means I don't have to *see* people.

Besides, I do see people anyway. I see them whenever I want. I can even see them now.

Sure enough, I look toward the distant lake, and after a moment I spot flickers of light moving along the shore. That's the road that stretches from Mannington to the north all the way down to Waverley. The flickers of light are reflected in the windows of cars making the journey, so each of those flickers represents a hot little vehicle filled with breathing, grunting, farting, smelling people going about their daily business. Don't get me wrong, I'm not a complete monster. I'm glad that people are out there, living their lives. I just don't want to have to deal with them.

I head back inside, while checking my mail.

As I step through the door, I hear a faint meowing and I glance down just in time to see Sheba hurrying into the house. I'm sure she had a great time last night, hunting in the forest, but she always comes home first thing in the morning. I think she waits nearby, watching the house for some sign of life. She probably understands now that I get up at 7am every single day. Today's Sunday, and I know a lot of people treat Sundays as if they're somehow different. For me, out here with just my cat for company, every day is the same.

"Are you hungry?" I say as I set the mail down unopened. I grab a box from the counter and head back out onto the porch, and I pour some food into Sheba's bowl.

Of course, half of yesterday's food is scattered nearby. Sheba's a messy eater, and she won't touch anything that's fallen out of the bowl.

"If you were more careful," I mutter, "you could have this inside."

Heading inside and setting the box back onto the counter, I note that it's getting quite empty. Fortunately my next food delivery is coming tomorrow, again in an automated vehicle. My order never changes. Sheba and I both have our habits. Once you've found something you like, why change?

I grab the letters again, figuring that I should just open them now rather than letting them fester.

As I head back to my desk, I glance at the television, which is running on mute. I shudder at the sight of thousands of people crowded into Central Park, and then I stop at the desk and remove the letter from inside one of the newly-arrived envelopes.

And then I freeze.

Glancing back at the silent television, I realize that the 'crowd' on the screen seems agitated. The camera shots are jerky and chaotic, as if something's happening. Feeling a flicker of dread in my chest, I realize that my fellow humans must have done something idiotic again. I watch the screen for a moment longer, but the red banner at the bottom of the image merely mentions the location. My first thought is that this must be the result of some terrorist attack, and then it occurs to me that perhaps some political figure is trying to stir up a crowd. Then, I wonder whether perhaps this is just some kind of music festival, or a demonstration against something, or one of those revolting 'flash mob' things that I read about a few years ago.

But then the image changes again, and I see that there's a vast, bright light burning straight through the center of the park, just a few feet above the ground.

I tell myself that this peculiar sight is the result of some kind of lens flare, but then the camera view changes slightly and I see that there's actually a ribbon-like strip of lightning crackling in the air, suspended in front of the waiting crowd.

Maybe I accidentally switched to a movie channel by accident.

"Sound on," I say, and the volume immediately turns up to its pre-set level.

"I don't know if they're still telling people to stand back," a reporter announces breathlessly, "but if they are, no-one's listening. It's as if the whole city has come to see this thing. I'm standing about a quarter of a mile back from where it starts, and I can tell you that there's no noticeable heat in the air. Whatever that thing is, it does seem to be getting a little taller, and we're getting unconfirmed reports that some people are seeing shapes and shadows in its center."

"Channel information," I say, and sure enough the ident pops up, proving that this is the news channel. It's not some wacky sci-fi movie that I've stumbled across by accident.

This is really happening.

As the camera view changes again, I realize I can hear an immense crackling sound coming over the speakers, along with the sound of helicopters and sirens. New York looks to be in the grip of utter chaos, and after a moment I step closer to the television as I try to get a better look at the *thing* that's filling Central Park. I tilt my head slightly, telling myself that I must be looking at some kind of strange weather effect, but deep down I'm pretty sure that this isn't the explanation.

"As for the length of this ribbon of light," the reporter continues, "we're hearing that it's opening up all across the North American continent, and perhaps even down into the central region. That makes it potentially more than a thousand miles long, and growing by the second. We're also -"

Suddenly she's drowned out by the sound of a huge roar from the crowd, and the camera starts shaking. For a moment, the visuals are completely frantic, and then the image cuts to a shot from a different angle. The camera zooms in wildly, struggling to maintain a coherent image, and the whole screen is filled with a shot of the ribbon. For a moment, all I can see is crackling white light, but then – as the crowd continues to scream and shout – I realize that there seems to be something moving deep in the heart of the energy.

I squint and step closer, peering at the television.

Sheba purrs and brushes against my legs.

"Quiet, honey," I whisper, tilting my head again as the shapes become clearer. After a moment, I start to understand what I'm seeing, although I can't quite believe that I can possibly be right.

But there are more of them now, emerging from the heart of this dancing ribbon of energy. I can just about make out their silhouettes now, and it's clear that they're walking on normal legs, with normal arms at their sides. I lean even closer, until the image starts to break into the individual dots on the screen, and at the same time the sound is getting louder and louder, so loud that the speakers of my television sound as if they could be about to explode. And then even louder, building to a crescendo as more and more figures emerge from the light.

People. There are people coming out of that thing.

CHAPTER TWO

Six months later...

"DAMN IT!"

Stumbling through into the kitchen, I somehow manage to bump against the wall. I reach out to steady myself, and in the process I knock several files and folders off the counter, sending paperwork flying out across the floor. I don't have time to gather it all up, not right now, so I step around the mess and head over to the window.

I freeze, staring out at the yard, listening for any hint that they're coming.

All I can hear is silence. Even the trees are remaining still. A moment later, I hear a faint bumping sound coming from nearby, followed by a faint meow.

AMY CROSS

"Quiet!" I hiss, not even turning to look at Sheba.

I need to think, but my mind is racing. I take a step back, only for my right foot to nudge something on the floor. Looking down, I see the dirty plates from last night's dinner, with pale sauce already dribbling over and spreading a puddle across the floor. I watch for a moment as the puddle reaches a pile of unopened mail. And then, suddenly, I hear a faint sound in the distance.

I turn and look out the window, and then I drop down onto my knees. My chest is so tight with fear, I can barely even manage to breathe. I reach out and place my hands against the window, while staring at the gravel road, but there's no sign of movement out there and the sound – which might not have been a sound at all – has stopped.

Where are they?

I know they're coming.

Today's the day.

Then again, what if something changed? I take my phone from my pocket. My hands are trembling, but I quickly see that I have no messages. That doesn't necessarily mean that they're still coming, however.

What if they changed their minds?

What if the rules have been changed?

What if they had an accident on the way here?

I feel bad for that last thought, but I don't want them to actually get hurt. I just want them to be delayed, for long enough that this stupid rule will get changed. Sanity has to prevail, people can't seriously think that this is the best solution to what happened. They've had six months to come up with an answer, six months to avoid their stupid knee jerk response. The Rutherford Act is ridiculous, and one of the legal challenges has to succeed eventually. I just need a little more time, until the world comes to its senses.

I crawl around the sofa and make my way behind one of the armchairs, and then I peer out over the top and once again watch the yard.

They're late.

They were supposed to be here one hour ago. They haven't called to say that they're late, and Donna's always on time, which means that obviously they're not coming. If they were coming, they'd have called to let me know that there's been a delay. Donna's always very polite like that, and very punctual. The fact that they haven't called means that obviously there's been an unexpected hiccup, and that in turn means that they almost certainly won't come today.

There.

That's sorted.

They're not coming.

Still, I can't quite bring myself to believe

that I'm this lucky. There was nothing on the news this morning about the Rutherford Act getting repealed. In fact, there were loads of news reports about how the Rutherford Act is being implemented, but I guess it's possible that the media outlets don't have all the information. I start to sit up slightly, while still peering out at the yard and at the gravel road beyond, and I tell myself that I have to stay calm. I have to stay level-headed. I have to hold my nerve.

Suddenly I hear the sound of an engine, and a moment later Donna's car bumps into view from behind the trees.

Startled, I drop down behind the armchair. My mind is racing and I can feel my heart pounding in my chest. For a few seconds I can't even think; my mind is filled with a kind of white-hot panic. I know I should have been prepared for this moment, but somehow I managed to convince myself that it wouldn't actually happen. Worse, I think I came to believe that by preparing, I'd be making it feel more real.

I hear the car come to a halt, and then the sound of a door opening, and finally footsteps on the gravel.

Maybe she's alone.

In fact, as I listen to the footsteps approaching the front door, I realize that there's clearly only one person out there. Maybe she's come to tell me that the whole thing is off? That the Rutherford Act has been suspended, or that I've been given an exemption. That would only be fair, really. Surely they understand that I can't be interrupted. I moved out here to get away from people, and it's wholly unfair to impose on me like this.

Suddenly there's a knock at the door.

I hold my breath. Looking around, I realize that there's no way Donna will be able to see me if she peers through the window next to the door. I should have hidden somewhere better, but for now this spot will do. Hopefully she'll figure that I'm out, that I have better things to do than sit around and wait for her to show up. Still, it might be to my advantage to talk to her, especially if she's only come to let me know that I'm off the hook. I take a moment to figure out a plan, and then I realize that I need to take a look at the car.

I pause for a few more seconds, and then I begin to very carefully, very slowly crawl around the side of the armchair. I just need to get to the lounge window and peer out at the yard, and then I can check that my suspicions are correct. I have to pick my way past some dirty plates that I left piled next to the sofa, but finally I reach the window and I look out.

Immediately, I see that there's a figure sitting in the back seat of Donna's car.

But is it her?

I squint trying to see better, but the figure's really no more than a silhouette. I squint harder, and I lean closer to the window, but it's still impossible to tell exactly what I'm seeing. There's a possibility, of course, that this still isn't bad news. Perhaps Donna is delivering somebody else to another house nearby, and she merely dropped in here first to let me know that I'm exempt. I mean, there's a chance that that's what's happening. Yet as I continue to peer at the figure, I can't shake the feeling that its outline *does* look a little familiar.

I need time to think.

I turn to crawl back behind the armchair, but then I freeze as I see Donna standing at the back window, staring at me with an unimpressed expression.

CHAPTER THREE

"NO, YOU SEE I can't take anyone in right now," I continue, stumbling over my words a little as I try to explain the situation, "because it would be too disruptive. I think possibly I should be exempted on medical grounds."

"There are no exemptions being issued, Ann," Donna replies calmly, sitting at the other end of the dining table. "You know that."

"I do," I stammer, "but in this case, I think it's only fair to look at the broader picture and see how grossly unfair this all is."

"The Rutherford Act is -"

"I know all about the Rutherford Act," I add, interrupting her. "Believe me, I've read it all the way through, over and over again."

"Looking for loopholes?"

"Let me try to put this another way," I reply, before pausing to try to think of the best phrasing. "I think maybe I have a disability."

She raises a skeptical eyebrow.

"Some kind of extreme phobia of other people," I continue, "bordering on a kind of critical, pathological aversion to company. I mean, I think there's a strong chance that I'm allergic."

"To people?"

"I think you should run some tests."

"There's really no point," she replies. "Ann, you can't be allergic to people. And even if you were, it wouldn't get you out of this. The Rutherford Act -"

"I know the Rutherford Act inside out!" I snap desperately.

"The Rutherford Act is an international treaty," she says firmly, before sighing. "Ann, it's the only way. Six months ago, a portal opened between our world and a parallel universe in which -"

"I know," I tell her, cutting her off again. "Believe me, I know."

"I think you need reminding," she replies, "of the severity of the situation. Two billion refugees came pouring out through that portal, into our world. Two billion people, Ann. Running from the end of their own world, seeking safe haven here in our world. We were already struggling with the size of our global population, and then overnight two billion more people showed up." She stares at me, as if she thinks that I need this explaining again. "These people are parallel universe versions of people in our world. The only way to integrate them, at least for now, is for each of them to live and work with their respective versions here. And since one of those two billion people is a version of you, Ann, that means you have to take her in."

"No."

"No is not an option."

"But -"

"And in case you were wondering," she adds, "she's not very happy about it either. She tried to escape the processing facility five times. She claims she can live off the land."

Now it's my turn to sigh.

"I had to lock her in my car when we arrived just now," she continues, clearly exasperated. "She does not want to be here, any more than you want to take her in."

"Then don't bring her."

"Where should she go instead?"

"She wants to live off the land. Let her do that."

"I've helped integrate these people into homes all across the state," she replies. "I've seen first-hand that it's not easy. I've delayed bringing the other Ann here for as long as I can, to give you time to get used to the idea. But the thing is, people all over the world are facing the same situation as you, and they're getting on with it."

"That's not what the news said," I tell her. "You make it sound like everyone else is fine and dandy with what's happening."

"Ann -"

"They've been murdering each other!" I blurt out.

"There have been a few isolated incidents where the integration hasn't gone as planned. Overall, the Rutherford Act has been implemented extremely well. There's no way out of this, Ann. There's a parallel universe of you sitting in my car, and the time has come for her to move in with you. Now, as we discussed before, you won't be abandoned. I'll be coming for weekly visits to check up on the both of you, and to help you with things."

"I'll pay you."

She sighs again.

"I'll pay you," I continue, "to take her away."

"Bribery isn't going to get you anywhere."

"Do you have one?" I ask. "Have you got a parallel universe version of yourself moving in with you?"

"I do not," she replies.

"Then you don't know how it feels."

"I get it, Ann. You're a solitary person. The

other Ann is solitary too. She barely spoke to anyone at the processing facility, and believe me, the ride here was not pleasant. At one point, she tried to open the door and jump out."

"You should have let her."

She stares at me for a moment, before getting to her feet.

"Where are you going?" I ask.

"I'm going to fetch her. This conversation is at an end."

"If you bring her inside, I'll kill her!"

"No you won't, Ann," she says, sounding tired as she heads to the front door. "You've made a dozen threats already, and you're not going to go through with any of them. I appreciate that this situation is difficult for you, but you're going to get through it. We all are. It's the only way."

I hurry after her, but she's already out on the porch.

Stopping in the doorway, I watch as she heads down the steps, and then I look at the car. And then, suddenly, I spot a face scowling out at me from one of the vehicle's windows, and for a moment I'm frozen by that very familiar expression. It's like looking into a mirror.

I pull back and step out of view, just as a beeping sound indicates that Donna has unlocked her car.

A few seconds later, I hear muffled voices,

and then the sound of footsteps on the gravel. Two sets of footsteps this time, coming closer.

This is not fair.

I can't let this happen.

At the same time, I don't know what to do. I guess my only hope is to speak with Donna again, to make her understand that I can't be forced to have some kind of room-mate. This is my own house, I worked hard and I paid for it myself, and nobody has the right to tell me that I have to take someone in and let them live with me. Finally, filled with a kind of righteous anger, I turn and step into view, ready to tell Donna that she'll have to break the walls down if she wants to get anyone in here.

And then I freeze, as I see an exact copy of myself standing in the doorway, staring through at me.

CHAPTER FOUR

"SO THE WEEKLY MEETINGS will be on Thursdays," Donna explains calmly, as she turns to the next page of documentation, "and I'll expect to see both of you. I really don't want to hear excuses, not after I drive all the way out here. Messing about will only waste your time, and my time. I hope we can all act like adults."

She stares at me, as if she expects me to meekly promise that I'll be a good girl. I open my mouth, ready to make some kind of sarcastic comment, but then I glance to the other end of the table.

There she is.

Me.

Or rather, an alternate version of me.

The other Ann.

She's staring down at the table. When I first set eyes on her, I thought we were exact doubles, but now I'm starting to notice a few subtle differences. Her hair is a little different to mine, although she can't escape that natural fall to the left. Her eyes are the same color as mine, but there are rings under them, leaving dark shadows that mark slightly sagging skin. And she's thinner, too. In fact, she looks painfully thin.

"Do I need to go through the section of the act concerning rules?" Donna asks.

Turning to her, I see that she's still staring at me, as if she expects me to throw a tantrum at any moment. After a few seconds, however, she turns to the Other Ann.

"The chip in your arm," she begins to explain, "is there for your own safety, so that you -"

"I know," she says suddenly. Her voice is a little more gravelly than mine, but not by much.

"Believe it or not," Donna continues, "I've seen integrations start worse than this. I've seen people screaming at their doubles, even physically assaulting them. The fact that the pair of you are sitting here at this table is already a positive sign. It shows me that progress is possible."

I glance again at the other Ann. She's still staring at the table. Suddenly filled with panic at the thought that she might look at me, I turn back to Donna.

"You just need to give it time," she adds.

I want to scream. I want to tell her to get the other me away from here. At the same time, I'm worried about losing control in front of my double. My skin feels tingly, as if I'm physically reacting to our proximity, as if her very existence is making me feel nauseous. Is it possible that this closeness really might make me ill? I guess I can't suggest that to Donna, but it's something I should consider and monitor.

First, though, I need to figure out a way to get out of this situation.

"So," Donna says suddenly, getting to her feet, "I'll see both of you next week."

"What?" I gasp, bolting up from my seat.

"I have to get back," she continues. "You look panic-stricken, Ann. Trust me, in my experience it's best to just get on with things. The pair of you need time to get used to the situation. I know it must be scary right now but... trust me."

With that, she grabs her bag and heads toward the door.

"Wait!" I hiss, bumping against the table in my rush to follow her. "You can't go!"

"I've got a long drive ahead of me."

She opens the door, but I grab her arm and try to hold her back.

"There's been a terrible mistake!" I tell her, as I feel a rush of panic rising through my chest. "I live alone. I've lived alone since I left college. I've never wanted to live with anyone ever again. I need solitude!"

"We all have to do our bit right now, Ann".

She pulls away and heads out onto the porch.

I run after her and grab her arm again, this time as she starts making her way down the steps.

"I have rights!" I tell her.

She sighs and turns to me.

"I have human rights!" I continue. "I can't just have another person foisted on me like this!"

"You should try talking to her," she replies. "You have a few differences, you might find those interesting."

She pulls her arm away again, and heads out toward her car.

"No, listen!" I stammer, panicking more than ever as I run after her and grab her arm yet again. "I'll do anything! I'll give you anything, I'll say anything, I don't care, but you have to take her away from here!"

"There's nowhere else for her to go, Ann," she replies. "And if I might say so, you're being a tad histrionic here. This might not even be forever, but right now it's the only way to organize the world."

"That's easy for you to say," I spit back at her. "You don't have your own double moving in with you. You're one of the lucky ones who doesn't have a double at all. You can just tell other people that this is their problem, and then you walk off laughing and you go back to your normal life and you don't care at all!"

"Ann -"

"You *don't* care!" I snap, unable to hold myself together any longer. "Look at you! You think this is funny!"

"No, Ann, I don't."

"Yes, you do! You're waltzing off home without a care in your mind, and you think I'm just supposed to turn my life upside down for that *thing* in there! And it's all just a joke to you, because you don't actually have to deal with it yourself! You don't actually know what it's like to feel this... panic in your chest! To have a doppelganger moving in with you and ruining your life!"

I wait, breathlessly, for her to admit that I'm right. I've got tears in my eyes, and I'm honestly not sure what else I can do or say to convince her that this has to stop.

"You're correct about one thing, Ann," she says finally, with a hint of sadness in her voice, "I don't know what it's like. I was one of the five and a half billion people who didn't have a doppelganger show up from a parallel universe. And do you what that means? It means my doppelganger in that other world didn't make it. She died in the war that broke out there." She pauses, and now there seem to be tears in *her* eyes too. "So yes, I don't have to take anyone in. But believe me, I'm not laughing about it. Because I know why I don't have to."

I open my mouth to reply, but for a moment I'm lost for words.

She pulls her arm free and climbs into her car, and then she pulls the door shut. I watch as she starts the engine, and then I feel a growing sense of hollow horror as she drives away. Tears are running down my cheeks, and I simply stand and watch as Donna's car disappears around the corner, and then I wait and listen to the sound of her engine getting further and further away, until finally all I can hear is the sound of nearby trees rustling in a faint breeze.

A moment later, hearing a board creaking on the porch, I turn and see the other me coming out of the house.

She stops and looks at me for a moment, and then she comes down the steps with her backpack over her shoulder and walks straight past me.

"Goodbye," she says as she heads out onto the road.

CHAPTER FIVE

"WAIT!" I CALL OUT. "Where are you going?"

She stops and turns to me.

"You don't want me here," she replies calmly, "and I don't want to be here, so there's a really easy solution. I waited until Donna left, and now I'm on my way. I figured I'd act co-operative while she was here. I'm not really big on pointless rebellion. I'd rather do whatever makes my life easier."

She hesitates for a moment.

"I guess you're probably the same," she adds, before turning to walk away. "Anyway, like I said, goodbye."

"Where are you going?" I ask again.

She stops – again – and turns to me.

"Where do you think?" she replies. "I'm

going to live in the forest. I don't know about you, but I've always been into foraging and agriculture. Growing stuff, that sort of thing."

"Me too," I tell her.

"Exactly. So I'll be fine. Goodbye."

She turns and walks away again.

"What about Donna?" I shout. "She's coming next Thursday. If you're not here, she'll send people to find you, and you've got a tracker."

"I know." She turns to me. "Sorry, I assumed you'd have automatically had the same idea that I had. I'll only be a few miles away. Far enough that we never have to meet, but close enough that every Thursday I can come back and sit around for a few hours, lying to Donna about how great you and I are getting on. Sure, it's inconvenient, but it's better than any of the other options. As for the tracker, I happen to know that it's been outsourced to a third party, and it's a nightmare for them to access the information."

"Are you sure?"

"I'm sure. On top of that, they have so much paperwork already, they don't want any extra. Trust me, Donna and everyone else in her position will do anything to avoid filling in extra forms. So, again, goodbye."

She half turns to leave, and then she hesitates.

"See you on Thursday," she adds.

With that, she walks away. I watch as she crosses the road, and then as she tramples into the forest and disappears from view. I can hear her footsteps for a little longer, but then even those die away, and I'm left standing all alone.

"Huh," I say finally, and what else *is* there to say?

That was so easy. She's gone. Problem solved.

***

"Honestly," the woman on the TV says as I finish wiping the dining table, "it's like I have a new best friend. Isn't that weird? It feels like it should be, like, egocentric or something, but it's not at all. We just have so much in common. Why shouldn't we get along?"

Glancing at the screen, I see a blonde woman sitting next to her exact double. This is another of those shows – so popular of late – about how people are managing to integrate their parallel universe counterparts into their lives. I know this kind of show is just meaningless dross, and I've begun to suspect that it's deliberate propaganda designed to make this whole situation more palatable to the viewing public. At the same time, I can't stop watching. I just don't understand how people can accept what's happening.

"We go everywhere together," the woman continues, as the shot changes to show them walking along the street, laughing and joking with one another. "We have the same taste in music and films and fashion. She is literally the perfect companion. I can barely remember what my life was like before she arrived."

"Freak," I mutter, before stepping back and looking around the room.

It's almost midnight, and I've been working non-stop all afternoon, but I've finally cleaned the house and put everything back to how it should be. I have to admit, over the past six months I've really let myself go, and I've been worrying constantly about how I'd deal with the arrival of my doppelganger. When I received a letter three months ago, confirming her existence and informing me of my duties under the Rutherford Act, I panicked completely, and the house became a dump. Now that my doppelganger has effectively tided herself away, however, I guess life can start to get back to normal. The house is spotless.

This is perfect.

Hearing a meowing sound outside, I glance toward the back door and realize that Sheba's out there. I've been so preoccupied all afternoon, I barely even noticed that she was out, so I head toward the door and slide it open. Sheba immediately shoots inside and starts brushing against my legs, and it's clear that she's pleased to see me. The sentiment is very much mutual.

"Hey," I say, reaching down and giving her a stroke, "I'm sorry Mommy's been a little out of sorts lately. I've had a lot on my mind, but it's going to be okay now. Are you hungry?"

I head to the counter and grab the box of food, and then I make my way out onto the porch. It's a cold night, and I feel pretty chilly as I lean over and pour food into Sheba's bowl. There are plenty of chunks that have been left spilled on the boards, but of course my fussy little cat would never dream of eating those. She has standards!

"There you go," I say as I stand up, and she immediately starts eating. "You're hungry tonight, huh?"

I turn to go back inside, but then suddenly I freeze as I look out across the dark yard and see the trees ahead. For a moment I stare into the void, and I can't help but think about the vast expanse of forest that spreads for miles and miles in every direction. My doppelganger is out there somehow, trying to eke out her existence. If she's anything like me – which I guess she is – she's spent most of her life developing the necessary skills, and she'll be fine. In fact, I imagine she'll be pretty happy living in the wilderness. I guess I should have realized that she'd hate the idea of moving in with me.

If our situations were reversed, I'd feel the

same way.

Again, I turn to go back into the house, but I stop again and look out at the forest. This time something feels different. I've been living here for several years now, and I've always loved being so far from civilization. Tonight, however, for the first time ever I feel as if I'm being watched. I can't see anyone out there in the darkness, and I can't hear anyone either, but I swear I can feel a pair of eyes staring straight at me, watching me intently. I tell myself that this is impossible, that I'm imagining things, yet the sensation only grows with each passing second. Finally, I start to feel as if I'm on the verge of a panic attack.

Stepping forward, I stop at the edge of the porch and peer out into the darkness.

"Hello?" I say finally, before I can stop myself. "Is anyone there?"

For a moment, I imagine *her* watching me. When the other Ann said she was going far out into the wilderness, maybe she wasn't being entirely truthful. Maybe she's sticking close to the house. Then again, why would she do that? She clearly had no desire to hang around, and I realize after a few seconds that I'm just allowing myself to become paranoid. After everything that has happened over the past six months – and today in particular – I guess that's not even much of a surprise.

Forcing myself to get a grip, I head back

inside. I slide the door shut and then – for a change – I pull the drapes across.

CHAPTER SIX

One week later...

DONNA'S CAR BUMPS TO a halt in the middle of the yard, and a moment later she pushes the door open and steps out.

"Hey there," she says with a smile. "How are things going out here?"

"Fine," I reply, watching from the top of the steps as she approaches the porch. "You're a little earlier than I expected. I didn't think you'd be here until after lunch."

"I didn't have anything on this morning," she says, coming up to join me. Already, she's conspicuously looking past me, as if she's waiting to spot the other Ann. "So, then. How's it going?"

I open my mouth to reply, but for a moment

I'm not quite sure what to say. The past week has been fairly calm, and I've mostly been able to get on with my work. I still felt as if I was being watched several times, mostly in the evenings, but I was gradually able to put that sensation out of my mind and focus instead on getting some work done. All in all, I think the week has been remarkably successful. I've felt less stressed that at any point since all of this madness started.

There's only one problem.

"So where is she?" Donna asks.

"Who?" I snap back, trying to seem relaxed.

"Your cat," she replies, before rolling her eyes. "Who do you think, Ann? Come on, I need to see both of you, to check how things are going and determined whether you need extra support."

She slips past me and starts making her way up the steps, toward the open front door.

"Maybe we should wait out here for a moment," I say, hurrying after her.

"And why's that?"

"It's a nice day."

She stops and turns to me, and I can immediately see that she's starting to become suspicious. She looks me up and down for a moment, then she turns and peers into the house, and then she turns to me again.

"Where is she?" she asks again. "Ann, you know I can have someone access the tracker, if that's what it takes. I want complete honesty from you, and nothing less."

"Well, you see..."

"Where is she, Ann?"

I hesitate. How do I explain this?

Suddenly I hear a bumping sound from inside the house, and Donna and I both turn to see the other Ann standing next to the dining room table. I guess she must have slipped in through the back door.

"Hello, Donna," she says calmly, as if nothing's amiss. "Sorry, I was in the bathroom. I didn't hear you arrive."

***

"She's made me feel completely at home," the other Ann says a short while later, as the three of us sit at the table. "Much more so than I ever could have imagined. She's been very gracious."

"Uh-huh," Donna replies, making a note on her pad before casting a skeptical glance at me. "That's very good to hear."

"What can I say?" I reply, forcing a thin smile. "I mean, I didn't want to be rude."

"I've mostly spent my time exploring the area," the other Ann continues. "It's the same as where I lived back in my world, of course, but there are a few very small differences. Plus, I know for a fact that my home back there was destroyed in one of the attacks, so it's nice to see it again after all this time." She looks about, as if she's genuinely marveling at the site of the house's interior. "It's like a blast from the past."

"What about tensions?" Donna asks. "You must have had some disagreements."

"No," we both say at the same time.

I glance at the other Ann.

She glances at me.

"There has to have been something?" Donna continues. "You're both... How can I put this? You're both used to living alone. This has been a big change for you. There must have been a little friction."

I look over at the other Ann, waiting for her to answer.

"I think space is the key," she says finally, and she sounds pretty convincing. "We don't get in one another's way very much. Or at all, really." She turns to me. "Isn't that right?"

"Absolutely," I reply, and I have to admit that I'm relieved she's taking the lead. She seems to have thought ahead, whereas I spent all morning worrying that there was no sign of her. "We've definitely found a way of living that works for us."

"So I see," Donna says, with a hefty dose of skepticism in her voice. She stares at me for a moment, then at the other Ann, and then she makes some more notes on her pad.

I crane my neck to subtly take a look at what she's writing. Without turning to me, she tilts the pad away so that I have no chance of seeing.

"I need to speak to each of you individually," she says after a moment. "Who'd like to go first?"

I open my mouth to say that I'll go out and play with Sheba for a few minutes.

"I'll go outside and play with Sheba for a few minutes," the other Ann says, getting to her feet. "It's weird, I had a cat in my world, but I named her Constance. It's funny how there are these little differences, isn't it?"

She heads toward the back door, and I notice once again that she's limping quite heavily on her right foot. She was fine last week, when she arrived, but since she showed up today she seems to have been carrying an injury. Not that she's said anything about getting hurt out there in the forest, but it's clear that something must have happened.

After a moment I turn and see that Donna is staring at me with a very suspicious expression on her face.

"Is everything alright?" I ask.

"You two are getting along very well," she replies.

"I thought that was what you wanted."

"I did. I mean, I do. It's just..."

Her voice trails off.

"Well," she adds finally, "I suppose this should be a lesson. Sometimes people surprise you. And I don't mind admitting, Ann, that you and the other Ann have *really* surprised me."

"Thanks," I reply with a smile. "You're welcome."

"There's just one other thing I need to ask you about," she continues, "and I couldn't do it while she was here." She sets her pen down. "Obviously all the people who came through the portal were fleeing a version of our world in which some pretty bad things had happened. I know you know the basics, about the war and the mass deaths. One of the things we're concerned about is the ongoing mental and emotional well being of these people. Ann, have you noticed anything about the other Ann that makes you worry?"

"Like what?"

"You read the leaflet I gave you, didn't you? The one about PTSD?"

"Oh, sure," I reply, and it's true. I *did* take a quick look. "No, I haven't noticed anything."

"She seems fine?"

"As far as I can tell."

She makes some more notes.

"Does she talk about it much?" she asks.

"No."

"Have you asked her about it?"

"No."

"Has it come up at all?"

"No."

She glances at me again.

"We don't have long conversations," I explain, trying to keep this whole thing from seeming too easy. Too suspicious. "Mostly we just get on with things. With our lives." I pause, waiting for another question, but she continues to stare at me. I need to say something more, but I'm not sure what. I feel as if I'm on the spot here. "I guess we just learned to compromise," I add finally. "She knows what she wants, and I know what I want, and we've found a way to make it work."

I wait.

Still, Donna is eyeing me with suspicion.

"So," I continue, "should I go outside and send her in?"

CHAPTER SEVEN

"SHE'S ONTO US," I say as a short while later, as we both stand on the porch and watch Donna's car disappearing into the distance. "What kind of questions did she ask you?"

"It was mostly about everyday life," she replies. "Don't worry, I managed to keep up the charade. I think she was surprised by how well things seemed to be going, but she was happy enough. I guess she'll take anything that means her paperwork's easy."

She pauses, before starting to limp down the steps. As she goes, she has to hold onto the railing.

"Are you okay?" I ask. "What happened?"

"It's nothing."

"You're hurt."

"It's nothing I can't walk off," she replies as

she starts limping slowly across the yard. "I told Donna I slipped, which is basically the truth. I just didn't tell her that I was five miles away at the time. It's a good job that tracker's not being constantly monitored, but I guess they can't afford stuff like that. Anyway, I'll see you next Thursday."

I almost call out to her, to offer her some lunch, but fortunately I managed to stop myself at the last moment. By some miracle, we've found an arrangement that works for us both, and I guess it would be foolish to start messing with that? What was the saying I learned from my grandfather? That's right: If it ain't broke, don't fix it. Apart from her limp, the other me seems perfectly happy out there in the forest, so I simply watch as she disappears back into the undergrowth.

"See you next week," I whisper, before turning and heading back into the house.

**

Thunder rumbles again, high above, and the electric lights flicker. I turn and look over toward the window, and for a moment I listen to the sound of rain pouring down outside.

"Michael Wallace thought he was doing the right thing when he accepted his double into his home," the voice-over on the TV says. "Twenty-four hours later he was dead, with his throat slit from side to side."

I turn back to look at the screen, and I wince as soon as I see a photo of a trashed house. It takes a moment before I realize that there's a dead body in the shot too, almost buried in the mess.

"After spending three days on the run," the voice-over continues, "Michael's doppelganger from another universe was finally apprehended."

Cut to a shot of a ragged, deranged-looking man staring straight at the screen.

"Michael Wallace's doppelganger," another voice says, before a shot of a psychiatrist sitting in her office, "was introduced into Michael's home under the auspices of the Rutherford Act, but scant attention was paid to the doppelganger's personality and mental state. And that's one of the real, fundamental problems of the Rutherford Act. It puts people together without taking the time to determine whether this is safe, and the result is a wave of killings that has claimed the lives of ordinary, decent people like Michael Wallace."

I slip another potato chip into my mouth as I continue to stare at the screen.

"Tonight," the narrator announces, "on *Doppelgangers Gone Bad*'s one hundredth edition, we bring you the most shocking case to date. And we ask whether the Rutherford Act is a request for kindness, or an invitation to kill."

The music ramps up and the title sequence

AMY CROSS

begins. I root around in the bowl, trying to find a really big, curly potato chip, and then I look at the window again as I hear rain falling harder than ever. If anything, the storm out there seems to be getting worse and worse with every passing minute, to the point that the sound of rain and wind is actually competing with the TV for my attention.

"Mute sound," I say out loud finally, and the TV falls silent.

Getting to my feet, I slip past the sleeping Sheba – who once again is proving that she can sleep through anything – and head to the window. It's gone midnight, and this storm really seems to have settled in for the night. There was no mention of a storm on the forecast this morning, but rain is crashing against the window and I can hear water gushing from the gutter than runs past the bathroom ceiling.

This is not a good night to be stuck out there in the forest.

Then again, she'll have shelter sorted by now. That would have been her first task when she went out there a week ago. I don't know what was in her backpack, but I wouldn't be surprised if she planned ahead and brought some kind of material that she can fashion together into a small but useful covering. I'd certainly have tried to do something like that, and I'd also have made sure to be wearing sturdy, waterproof boots. I know everyone at the

62

processing center was given a small budget with which to buy certain necessaries, and I'm sure that the other Ann would have used this money extremely wisely.

I remember going camping when I was a kid. We lived near my cousins, and sometimes a whole swarm of relatives would descend on us, filling our house with yells and pushing and shoving. My parents knew how much I hated all of that, so they'd let me take my tent and go stay out in the garden for the duration. They even turned a blind eye whenever I moved my tent just a little beyond the garden, onto the wasteland near our house. They knew I was safe, and that I could look after myself, and also that I'd be much happier with peace and solitude. So, really, the other Ann is just doing her version of the same thing. Both of us are better off.

I stare out at the storm for a moment longer, before turning and heading to the sofa.

The TV is on mute, but the screen is showing flashing images of a smiling, happy man.

"Sound on," I say as I sit back down and set the bowl of potato chips back on my lap.

"His was a contented life," the voice-over says darkly, as the images continues, "and he made a positive contribution to his community. But Michael Wallace's life was to change forever when he learned that he had a doppelganger from another dimension. From that moment on, Michael Wallace was marked for death."

I slip another potato chip into my mouth, as the screen shows images of a bloodied hallway. There's an arc of blood on the wall, obviously sprayed from a severed human jugular.

CHAPTER EIGHT

One week later...

"I'M COMING," I mutter, taking one more sip from my morning coffee before grabbing the box of cat food and heading toward the back door. "Keep your panties on."

Sheba's really making a noise out there this morning. I've been busy doing a spot of cleaning, since today's Thursday and Donna's due for her next weekly visit. As I slide the door open and step out onto the back porch, I'm already making mental notes of a few more things that I need to get done. I glance toward the forest, but I know the other Ann isn't likely to show up yet, and then I turn and reach down to pour food into Sheba's bowl. The poor cat is still meowing loudly.

"Huh," I say suddenly, as I see that something's different this time.

Usually, there's plenty of discarded food around Sheba's bowl. My fussy old cat won't eat anything that she's spilled, but this time there's not so much as a crumb left either inside or close to the bowl. I look around, in case the stray crumbs have been knocked somewhere, but the decking is completely clear.

Sheba bumps against my leg, as if she's urging me to get on with things.

"You're really hungry today, huh?" I say, before starting to pour. Uncharacteristically, Sheba ducks under my wrist and starts eating even before I've finished filling the bowl. "Calm down," I continue. "Anyone would think you haven't eaten in days."

***

"I'm sure she'll be here real soon," I tell Donna as we sit at the dining room table. "I really don't know what's kept her. She only went out for a walk."

Donna stares at me, not looking particularly impressed, and then we both turn and look at the empty chair where the other Ann would usually be sitting.

I glance toward the back door, hoping against hope that I'll suddenly hear footsteps approaching the house, but there's nothing. Next, I look at the window, and I watch the forest for a moment.

Is this some kind of game?

Is the other Ann waiting and lurking, planning to step out at the last moment? Perhaps she simply wants to make me sweat. On the other hand, is it possible that she's decided to run away? I can't possibly be held responsible for her actions, but I know that under the terms of the Rutherford Act she'll simply be tracked down, hauled back and detained on my property more forcefully. I've heard rumors that some repeat offenders have even been physically chained in rooms for weeks at a time, as punishment.

Damn her, if she's done something stupid that results in her getting chained inside my house.

"Is there anything I need to know?" Donna asks.

Turning to her, I can see the skepticism in her eyes.

"No," I say, figuring that it's in my best interest to simply play dumb. "Honestly! She went for a walk!"

"And she does that a lot, does she? She goes for walks?"

I nod.

"But she always comes back?"

I nod again.

"And she's aware that I was due to come today?"

"Uh huh. Definitely."

"I see."

She bites her bottom lip for a moment, before looking over at the window and waiting. We sit in silence for a moment, and then she looks down at her watch. Finally, she starts jotting down some notes on her pad.

"I'm as surprised as you are," I say, keen to stress my lack of culpability in this situation. "I mean, it's not like I'm her keeper. I can't be expected to watch her all the time."

"You can't, no," she replies, but she still doesn't sound too impressed as she makes more notes. "As long as you're being completely honest with me about your relationship with her, that's fine."

"Of course I'm being honest," I tell her. My mouth feels dry. "Why wouldn't I be being honest? What makes you think that I'm not being?"

She finishes her notes, and then she takes her pad and slips it into her bag.

"I'm going to level with you, Ann," she says finally. "I could call this in right now and get the ball rolling with a full search. There'd be teams with dogs here within a few hours, and a helicopter flying overhead, and I'd access the tracking information. That's what I'm supposed to do, but I have a little leeway. And the crazy thing is, I actually trust you."

"You do?" I ask, raising my eyebrows. "I mean, yes. You do. You should. I mean, you can."

She sighs.

"If this had happened a week ago, at my first return visit," she replies, "I'd have done all of those things and more. But I saw real progress last week, and I don't want to jeopardize that by injecting distrust into the situation. You say that the other Ann goes on walks like this regularly, and I believe you. I also understand that perhaps she's lost track of time, and none of that is your fault. So I'm going to hold back on reporting her absence this week." She stares at me for a moment, as if she's trying to read my mind. "Am I going to regret this act of leniency, Ann?"

I wait for her to continue, before suddenly realizing that she wants me to answer.

"Of course," I stammer. "I mean, no. You won't regret it."

"And she *will* be here next week?"

"Definitely."

"By hook or by crook?"

I nod.

"You'll make sure?"

"I will."

"Because if she's not, there'll be consequences. For her, and maybe for you if it turns out that you're lying to me."

I swallow hard.

"I'm not lying," I tell her, figuring that I'll come up with a plan once she's gone. "I don't know why she's late back, but I'll make absolutely certain that she's here next week."

"This is a big deal," she continues. "Don't let me down."

"Of course," I reply. "I mean, I won't. I promise. She'll be here next time, I swear."

I wait for her to reply, but she's just staring at me. As the seconds tick past, I feel more and more uncomfortable, and more and more as if I have to say something.

"You can count on me," I add finally, forcing a smile. "She'll be here next time. I'll make sure of that."

CHAPTER NINE

"DAMN IT!"

Stumbling as my foot catches against a tree root, I have to reach out and steady myself for a moment. There's been quite a bit of rain over the past week, and that's left the forest floor feeling very wet and mulchy. I usually don't come out at all when the terrain's this bad, but today I really can't help myself. Donna left an hour ago, and I'm already panicking at the thought of her returning next Thursday and the other Ann still not showing up.

She's out here somewhere.

I just have to find her and persuade her to cooperate.

"Hello!" I call out, cupping my hands around my mouth. "Where are you?"

I wait, but all I hear is silence.

Lowering my hands, I look out through the forest, watching the gaps between the trees and hoping for some sign of movement. I guess, in my mind's eye, I was hoping to quickly and easily stumble across a makeshift tent. I was hoping that this would be easy. Now, however, I'm starting to realize that there's mile after mile of forest stretching in every direction, and searching for the other Ann is like looking for a needle in a haystack. That's assuming she's even still in the area at all.

I set off again, struggling through the undergrowth and making much slower progress than I'd expected. Every few minutes, I stop and call out again, hoping against hope for some luck. And every few minutes, I feel another flicker of concern as I realize that there's still no sign of her.

Finally, after more than an hour, I reach the old path that winds up from the valley. Out of breath and feeling soreness in my legs, I stop and look out at the beautiful view. The lake is glittering down below in the afternoon sun, and I can just make out the glint of a few cars making their way along the coastal road. All around, the forest stretches out for what seems like an eternity. I love the view from here, I sometimes come out just to take a look, but today the view makes me feel a little uneasy since it's making me understand one very important thing.

If the other Ann really doesn't want to be found, then I have no chance. All I can do is wait and hope, and pray that next Thursday she shows up to meet Donna. Maybe this was just a little act of defiance. That's something that she – that *I* – definitely might do.

"Come on, don't be an obstinate asshole," I mutter under my breath, even though I know she can't hear me. "We're in this together. Let's not cause ourselves any more trouble than we already have to deal with."

Sighing, I turn and set off on the journey back toward the house. I'm starting to think that maybe I should have been honest with Donna, that maybe I should have admitted that I hadn't seen the other me for a while. Sure, I'd have had plenty of explaining to do, but at least I'd have a clear conscience, and at least there'd be no risk of her finding out later that I lied to her. The last thing I need is for penalty fines to start building up. It's not as if the other Ann could reimburse me for any of that.

By the time I'm halfway back to the house, I'm desperately out of breath and I have to take a moment to rest. I had no idea I was getting so out of shape, but I guess the past six months have been pretty hectic. I was so busy frantically reading about the Rutherford Act, and trying to find a loophole, that I barely had time to eat. On top of that, Donna started showing up to prepare me for the other me's eventual arrival, and I honestly don't think that I went on a single hike in all that time. I definitely need to get back to that. I still need to live my life.

Once I've caught my breath again, I set off to complete the journey, but after just a few steps I spot something nearby.

Stopping, I peer through the forest, and finally I realize that there's a patch of fabric that has been suspended between three trees, forming a kind of crude, low canopy.

Realizing that I must have found the other Ann's hideout, I take a step forward, but then I stop again as I realize that she might be nearby. I want to find her, of course, but I also don't want her to think that I've been worried. If she deliberately avoided coming to see Donna today, then maybe she's trying to get a reaction out of me, which means that she'll probably get a real kick out of seeing that I'm worried. I wipe sweat from my brow and try to figure out what I should do next, but I already know that there's no way I want to give her the satisfaction of a reaction. I need to prove a point here, so I guess I should just head back to the house and come up with a plan.

I take one final look around, just to make sure that the other me is nowhere to be seen, and then I start making my way around the edge of this impromptu campsite. I try to make as little noise as possible, but then I stop again as I realize I can see a pair of legs poking out from under the canopy.

It's her.

I can only make out the bare legs, with a pair of dark sneakers on the feet, but I'd recognize those slightly large thighs anywhere. They're my thighs – I mean, they're *her* thighs. I mean... I know what I mean. Anyway, she seems to be flat on her back, and she's not moving at all. I guess maybe she's sleeping, although after a moment I realize that her legs look quite dirty, with spots of mud and other crap all over, especially around the knees.

And then I spot the bowl.

There's a metal bowl on the ground, close to her left foot. The bowl is filled with water, and I immediately realize that the other me must have been trying to collect rainwater. That's a good idea, except that the bowl is over-filled and even from here I can see some dirt floating on the surface. If she's anything like me, the other Ann would keep that bowl scrupulously clean.

I turn to continue my journey back to the house, but then I freeze again as I realize that something feels wrong here. I stare at the legs, and I tell myself that I'll leave just as soon as I see some hint of movement. Sure, she seems to be asleep, but eventually she'll twitch or groan or move for some other reason.

As soon as I see that she's okay, I'll sneak

off.

CHAPTER TEN

GASPING, I FINALLY REACH my front room, and I drop to my knees as I struggle to set the other Ann's motionless body onto the sofa. My arms and legs are killing me after carrying her all the way back here, but my heart is pounding and I'm already checking once more for any sign that she's going to wake up.

I check her pulse, which felt weak back in the forest. She's definitely alive, but her eyes haven't opened since I found her and her skin is sickly pale color. I put a hand against her forehead and feel that she's very cold and clammy, and I have to brush some matted hair from across her face. She seems to have been sweating quite heavily, and her clothes are damp.

Looking down at her feet, I see that her right

ankle still looks swollen. I take one more look at her face, just to make sure that she's not stirring, and then I crawl to the other end of the sofa and start to very carefully untie the laces on her right sneaker. I'm no doctor, I don't have a clue what I'm doing here, but I work slowly and tentatively until I'm finally able to start slipping the sneaker off. I was half expecting her to let out a pained cry during this process, but she remains unconscious even as I pull the sneaker aside and expose a horribly red, misshapen ankle.

She must have really hurt herself out there.

I touch the side of the ankle and find that the skin feels warm. I twisted my ankle a few times as a kid and it was painful, but at least I had Mom around to give me some ice and generally take care of me. I'm not an expert, but it looks to me as if the other Ann twisted her ankle and then just tried to leave it to heal. Judging by the swelling and the redness, however, I imagine she got to the point where she could no longer walk. Stuck out there in the forest, all alone and with no means of communication, she would have been in real danger. And that's before the terrible weather that's swept through the area in waves over the past week.

Stumbling to my feet, I hurry into the kitchen, ignoring Sheba's meows. I grab a bottle and fill it with water, and then I head back over and kneel once more next to the other me. I really don't know what else to do, so I tilt her head to one side and part her lips, and then I try to force her to drink.

***

My phone is resting on the kitchen counter. It's been resting there all afternoon, and I've been staring at it for the best part of an hour. I keep telling myself that I don't need to call for help, that an ambulance would be overkill, but I'm also very much aware that evening is approaching. Given the perilous nature of some of the roads around here, I need to make a decision soon. If I don't call for help within the next half hour or so, we risk being cut off for the night.

Finally, telling myself that I have to do the right thing, I reach out for the phone.

Suddenly I hear a creaking sound coming from the front room, and I turn just as the other Ann lets out a faint, pained groan.

Hurrying to the doorway, I look through and see that she's trying to sit up on the sofa, although she seems disorientated and a little dazed. She doesn't seem to have noticed me, and for a moment I simply watch as she reaches out and mumbles something under her breath. And then, before I can stop her, she suddenly rolls onto one side and tumbles off the side of the sofa, landing hard on the floor and crying out as her damaged ankle hits the side of the nearby armchair.

"Steady!" I say, hurrying over to help. "It's okay, you're safe! I found you and brought you here!"

She scrambles to get up, but she can't manage to haul herself off the floor. I take hold of her arms and try to steady her, but she seems to be in something of a panic, and it takes a few seconds before she looks up at me. Finally she freezes, and I see the moment of realization in her eyes as she slowly turns and looks around the room.

"I found you in the forest," I tell her, still supporting her so that she doesn't slump back down. "You were pretty sick, I was about to call an ambulance. I think you had a fever, something like that. It looks like you've hurt your ankle."

She turns to me, and then she looks down at her right foot.

"It's pretty badly swollen," I explain, even though that point is kind of obvious. "Looks like you twisted it bad. I'm trying to get some ice together, but it's not quite ready yet."

She murmurs something, but I can't quite make out the words.

I reach out to check the temperature of her forehead, but she pulls away.

"I'm trying to help," I tell her. "That's all."

She stares at me for a moment, and she looks utterly terrified. I'm not even sure that she understand where she is, and I'm starting to think that this fever is affecting her thought process.

"It's me," I continue, somewhat unnecessarily. "I'm going to help you back onto the sofa, okay?"

I wait for an answer, but she simply continues to stare.

"It's me," I say again. "I'm going to get you back up on the sofa."

I wait again, but finally I realize that I just need to get on with the job. She's clearly a little dazed still, but I'm sure she'll come around eventually, so I reach under her armpits and try to get a better grip, and then I start to haul her back up.

Suddenly something slams into the side of my head, not too hard but with enough force to startle me. Letting go of the other me, I pull back just as I'm hit again, and this time I see that the other me has grabbed her discarded sneaker and is trying to use it to beat me away.

"Stop!" I yell, holding my hands up to defend myself as more blows come raining down. "Hey, cut that out!"

She hits me again, but this time she loses her grip on the sneaker and it bounces off my face. I fall back and land flat on my ass, just as the other me turns and tries to get to her feet.

As soon as she tries to pressure on her injured right foot, she cries out and slumps back down, and then she starts crawling toward the back door.

Sheba bolts out from behind one of the other chairs and races, terrified, into my bedroom.

"Will you please calm down?" I shout as the other me slowly crawls across the rug. "I'm doing this for you, you idiot!"

She mutters something that I don't quite hear, and then she stops at the back door and reaches up toward the handle. She tries to pull the door open, but she seems too weak and after a moment she stops as if she's trying to come up with a better plan. I wait, not really knowing how to respond, and then finally she tries once again to stand. This time, she manages to almost balance on her left foot, only to slip at the last moment. As she slumps back down, she lands hard on her right ankle, and I wince as she lets out a cry of pain.

"Are you done now?" I ask.

I wait, but now I realize that she hit her head on the door's glass pane as she fell, and she seems to have fallen unconscious.

"Seriously?" I say after a moment, before hauling myself up onto the sofa and leaning back with a sigh. "See?" I continue. "This is what happens when I try to help people."

CHAPTER ELEVEN

MORE RAIN IS FALLING outside as I sit at the dining room table and check a set of designs on my laptop. I've done precious little work recently, and it's time I tried getting back into some kind of regular schedule. Fortunately my clients have been understanding, perhaps in part because a few of them have also had to take doppelgangers in under the terms of the Rutherford Act. I'm far from the only person in the world who's having to deal with this crap.

Hearing a murmur nearby, I turn and look over toward the other end of the room, and I see that the other me is finally stirring. She's been on the floor ever since she knocked herself out, and I didn't really fancy trying to move her again. Now she's stirring, and I watch as she sits up and looks around.

"Hey," I say finally, "are you going to hit me

with your sneaker again?"

She turns to me, and I'm relieved to see that she looks a little more normal, as if maybe the fog of confusion has lifted.

"It's over there," I continue, pointing past the sofa. "You can thank me later, by the way. For carrying you all the way back here and basically saving your life. You're welcome."

Hearing the pitter patter of little footsteps, I turn to see that Sheba has finally dared to come out of the bedroom. She stops and looks over toward the other me, and then she looks up at me and lets out a plaintive meow, as if she wants me to explain exactly what's going on.

"Hey," I say, reaching down and stroking the back of her neck, "don't stress. It's cool."

She meows again, before turning and heading back into the bedroom.

As the other me continues to sit on the floor, I get to my feet and make my way around the table. The constant tapping of rain on the glass is strangely comforting, and for the first time today I actually feel a little calm. I spent so long worrying that the other me had run away, and I have to admit that in some weird way I'm relieved to see her.

"So do you want me to help you back onto the sofa?" I ask. "It'll be a lot more comfortable than the floor."

She pauses, before shaking her head.

"Then what -"

"I have to go," she stammers, as she starts trying to get back to her feet. "I'm sorry."

I head over to help her, but she pushes me away. A moment later she bumps her right foot and gasps, and she totters forward. I manage to grab her at the last moment and keep her from falling, and then I support her weight and half help, half *force* her over and onto the sofa.

"I have to go," she says again, sounding distinctly irritated. "I can't stay here."

"You can't even walk," I point out.

"Where's my sneaker?"

"I told you, it's -"

"Give it to me!"

Realizing that she seems to be ignoring most of what I say, I step around the sofa and grab the sneaker, and then I hand it to her. She snatches it and reaches down to slip it back onto her foot, and I watch as she makes several attempts to slide the side over her swollen ankle. Each time, she gasps at the pain and has to stop, but she keeps on trying until finally she surrenders.

"It's wet," she says, "I'll just carry it and dry it out when I get back to my tent."

"You mean that bit of fabric you strung between some trees?"

"It's none of your business where I sleep."

"No offense, but you didn't seem to be doing

too well out there."

"I didn't ask for your opinion."

"I just want to help."

"I'm doing fine by myself."

"Sure you are. By the way, have you been sneaking onto my porch at night and eating my cat's food?"

She turns and glares at me, but it's the kind of glare that tells me I'm right.

"I'm not trying to butt in," I say, feeling as if this conversation is going round and round in circles, "but when I found you out there, you were in a bad state. If I'd been a day later, I think you might have..."

My voice trails off as I realize that I could well have gone out there and found her dead. That would have been weird. *Very* weird.

"I was doing just fine," she mutters darkly, as rain continues to fall outside. "I just had a spot of bad luck, that's all. I slipped and hurt my ankle, and that made it harder for me to find food and water. I'll be okay this time."

"Your ankle's still bust," I point out.

I wait, but she doesn't seem to have an answer for that.

"Listen," I continue, "I don't like the situation any more than you do. But you can't really walk, and I was about to make some pasta with cheese, and it's really no trouble to serve up a little extra."

"I don't need your charity."

"It's not charity, it's..."

I try to think of a suitable analogy.

"It's food," I say finally, "and I have some, and you don't, so I'm offering some. I don't know what your cooking skills are like, but mine pretty much suck. So it won't be some great culinary delight, but it'll be food and I'm guessing you must be pretty hungry."

I wait for an answer.

"Or," I add, "I could just bring you a bowl of kibble."

She turns and glares at me again.

"I'll go cook," I say diplomatically, taking a step back, "and I'll bring something through. I might also open a bottle of wine, which is a pretty bad habit of mine, but I'll bring you a glass of that as well. You're not a prisoner, you can leave any time you like, but I don't think the weather's going to get any better out there. I know I definitely wouldn't want to get soaked again. I can also find some clothes for you to change into, and I can dry what you've got on now." I wait for her to say something, but she's simply watching me. "Back soon," I add.

I turn and head through to the kitchen. As I go, I glance into my bedroom and see the Sheba is on my bed, staring out at me from the darkness. I know that cat well, and I swear she looks worried.

CHAPTER TWELVE

"I GUESS YOU KNOW the basics of the war," the other me says later, as she sits on the sofa with a bowl of pasta in front of her, watching me as I sit in the armchair. "You know what happened."

"I got the gist of it," I tell her, before blowing on my pasta in an attempt to cool it down a little. "Something about a post-apocalyptic nightmare?"

"I never thought it'd actually happen," she replies. "There were all these news stories about this country threatening that country and so on, but I always assumed that the people in charge were too smart to actually go through with any of it. I watched the news and rolled my eyes and waited for it all to pass, and occasionally there'd be a week or two without too much happening. Then one night there was news of some explosions in Washington and New York, and people started saying it was other countries attacking us via proxy, using terrorists, and everything unraveled from there. I think the first nuclear strike was about three days later."

"It sounds awful," I tell her, not really knowing what else to say.

"At first I thought I could sit it out," she continues. "I lived in this exact house, in my world. I thought I was far enough away that I could just wait for everything to get back to normal. But then society collapsed and people just went nuts, and one day..."

She pauses, and then she reaches up and touches her waist, as if she's feeling the knotted scars beneath the fabric of her shirt.

I want to ask exactly what happened, but I figure that maybe she doesn't want to tell me.

"A woman just came out of the forest one day," she continues, turning to look out at the window. Rain is still falling, but the porch light is just bright enough let us see the faintest hint of the trees at the far end of the yard. "She seemed friendly at first, she said she just wanted help. I didn't see the knife behind her back until it was too late. I'll never forget the feeling of it as it..."

Her voice trails off.

She stares into space for a moment, with her

hand still touching her waist, and then suddenly she turns and points out toward the porch.

"I staggered away and made it back inside," she explains. "What saved me was the fact that the knife stayed in the wound. If it had come out, the woman could have used it on me again, but I took it with me as I tried to get away. The other piece of luck was that it actually didn't cut anything vital, which is something of a miracle. Anyway, the woman came after me, trying to explain that it was nothing personal but that she just needed food for her family. She followed me over to the counter."

She turns and points toward the kitchen counter.

"She tried to grab the knife from me, but I'd left a steak knife on the side earlier in the afternoon. I took that and spun around, and there was a blur and somehow I sliced the thing straight into her chest. Right through her heart, I think. The look on her face was..."

Again, her voice trails off.

"I'm so sorry," I say after a moment, figuring that I should say *something*. "I can't imagine what it was like."

"I was terrified," she continues. "I took the knife out of my belly, I thought I'd most likely bleed to death right there and then, but again there was some kind of miracle. I managed to patch it up, and then I got my bike out of the shed and figured I needed to go and get help." She turns to me. "Do you have a bike?"

I nod.

"Is it green?" she asks.

"Red, actually."

"Huh." She stares at me. "It's funny how so much is the same, but there are these little differences."

"So you cycled away?" I continue. "Is that how you ended up coming through the portal?"

"I still don't quite understand all of that," she replies. "The world was rapidly becoming a nuclear wasteland, we all knew that we didn't have long. I ended up in Chicago, of all places, after hitching a ride with some guys who happened to go past me in their truck. Without them, I'd probably have died on the side of the road. I mean, I was weak from blood loss and it was only adrenaline that got me as far as I managed. And then, once we were in Chicago, these experimental bombs fell from the sky. That's what we heard, anyway. They were supposed to wipe us out, but when they exploded, something weird happened. The explosions kind of hung in the air, like sheets of light."

"I think scientists from our world still don't quite understand how the portal worked."

"It took a while before we realized we could pass through into another world," she explains. "At that point, it felt like we didn't really have much to lose, so..." She pauses. "Here I am. Along with two billion other people who escaped the same way."

"And now the portal's closed again," I point out.

"Exactly. We're stuck in your world, like refugees from another reality." She's still clutching the side of her neck as she turns and looks around again. "It's the same house I used to live in," she adds. "Almost down to every last detail. Even the decoration is the same, and most of the furniture. Your style's a little more flowery than mine, though."

"Flowery?" I raise a skeptical eyebrow. "Nobody's ever called me *flowery* before."

"I was thinking mainly about that vase," she explains.

"A present from an ex-boyfriend. An asshole named Peter."

"I never dated anyone named Peter."

"You didn't miss much," I tell her, and we both smile. "It must be weird for you, though. Being back, I mean. Back but not back."

"It's weird being a guest in my own home," she replies. "Feeling like I'm..."

Again, her voice trails off.

"You're welcome to stay for as long as you need," I say after a moment, surprising myself a little. "I know it's strange, and maybe I wasn't quite as welcoming as I could have been, but I have a lot of space here. You can stay and we don't even have to get in each other's way too often."

I wait for her to answer, but she seems uncomfortable. After a moment she starts looking around the room again, and I can't help but realize that for her this house must hold some very different memories. She already mentioned the day she was stabbed, and I imagine that a few other traumatic things happened during her final days here. Donna mentioned the possibility of PTSD, and as I look at the other me I start to wonder what else she might have seen during the war in her world. Maybe I'm imagining things, but I swear she looks slightly gaunt, with a haunted expression in her eyes. It's strange to see my face with a few subtle differences, and I stare at her until suddenly she turns to me.

"You're very kind," she says finally. "With the way my ankle is right now, I guess I don't have much choice. I'll help out around the place, though. I'm not a freeloader and I won't accept charity."

"It's not charity," I tell her, "it's... self help."

I smile, but she simply stares at me. I guess that little joke wasn't very funny.

"I'll sort you out with some bedding for the sofa bed," I continue, as I pick up my bowl of pasta and start swirling some around my fork. "I've had people stay a few times, and they've always said that it's really comfortable."

"I know," she replies as I begin to eat. "Me too."

CHAPTER THIRTEEN

RAIN IS STILL POURING down outside, running from the gutter, as I stare at the window. It's late, past midnight, and I've been trying to get to sleep for a few hours now. My mind is racing, however, and I can't help but stare across the pitch-black bedroom and watch the window. I keep telling myself that the constant rhythm of the rain will eventually lull me to sleep, but I'm not sure that's really true.

I feel more awake than I've ever felt in my life.

What if I said something stupid to the other me tonight? I keep going over and over our conversation, wondering whether I was insensitive or abrupt or rude. The more she talked, the more I began to realize that there are some major differences between us. Sure, we look the same, and we seem to have had pretty much identical lives for our first three decades. But then the war arrived in her world, and I think I might have underestimated just how much she was changed by all of that. I keep trying to imagine what it must have been like for her, but the truth is...

I don't think I *can* imagine it.

She has that big scar on her side, and a couple of other smaller scars too. She's definitely a little thinner than I am, and there are faint shadows under her eyes. I keep catching a kind of darkness in her eyes, though, and it's difficult to be sure how much of that is real and how much is in my imagination. When she told me about her experiences in the war in her world, the stories sounded horrific, but I'm also aware that she seemed to be holding a lot back. She told me about dead children she found in the streets, and about dying people she tried to help. She told me about being attacked, and she hinted that she might have had to kill a few people in order to survive. If those are the things she was willing to talk about, however, I can't even begin to imagine the rest. What *can't* see talk about? What's too dark, too awful?

And then there's her twitch.

It took me a while to notice, but the other me has a faint twitch on her right cheek. It's very subtle, but when she's talking about the war she sometimes gets this twitch that runs all the way up to the side of her eye. At first I thought I was imagining the whole thing, but this evening I realized that it was real. I can't ask her, of course, because she might not even be aware of it herself. But it's clear that there's a lot going on beneath her calm exterior, and I'm becoming increasingly worried that she might not be as 'okay' as she pretends.

I mean, I've always been good at hiding my feelings from other people. It's only natural that she should be the same.

Rolling onto my back, I decide to try this position again. I need to get some sleep at some point tonight, because I've got a feeling that my first full day with the other Ann in the house is going to be... interesting. I'm supposed to be working on something for a client, which will be tricky if I've got the other me resting on the sofa. Then again, I'm sure that she of all people will understand the situation, and it's not impossible that she'll be helpful. Closing my eyes, I try to tell myself that I'm letting my thoughts and fears run wild.

I take a deep breath.

I exhale, and then I inhale again.

And then, a moment later, I hear a creaking sound coming from near the bed.

Startled, I open my eyes and turn to look across the room, and I immediately see the figure of the other me silhouetted in the doorway. I sit up, and now my heart is racing, and I watch as the figure half turns to walk away.

"Sorry," she says, sounding exhausted, "I couldn't sleep so I just thought I'd take a look around."

I swallow hard, but I'm not quite sure how to reply.

"I didn't mean to wake you," she continues. "Just go back to sleep."

I wait, but she's still standing in the doorway.

"How long have you been there?" I ask.

For a moment, there's no reply.

"Not long," she says finally. "I should've waited until morning. I'm sorry. Go back to sleep."

I open my mouth to tell her that it's fine, but then she turns and limps out of sight. I listen to the sound of her going back into the front room, and I wait for the inevitable creak of the sofa as she sits down. The creak doesn't come, however, and instead I hear a different sound. I know I'm probably imagining things, but it sounds as if she's opening the drawer in my desk. A moment later, as if to confirm that suspicion, I hear the tell-tale sound of some paperwork being moved aside.

I hesitate for a few seconds, wondering what to do, and then I get to my feet.

After heading out of the bedroom, I stop and

look across the front room. Sure enough, the other me is sitting at my office chair, in front of my desk, quietly looking through various papers from the drawer. She's tilting each page in an attempt to see it better without turning on the light, and I watch as she carefully sets one page aside and takes a look at the next. It's quite clear that she's trying to be as quiet as possible. I mean, there's nothing bad in those files, there's nothing that I'm trying to hide from anyone. At the same time, it's unnerving to see the way that she's just casually looking through them as if they belong to her.

I briefly consider saying something, but I'm worried about her thinking that I'm a snoop. That's pretty ironic, considering what *she's* doing, but I figure I need to be a little diplomatic.

Stepping back, I head into my bedroom again.

I can still hear the other me in the front room. Every minute or so, I hear another piece of paper getting gently set aside. At first, I assumed that she was trying to be quiet, but now I realize that she might not even care. She knows that I'm awake, so she must understand that I can possibly hear her. I guess maybe she just doesn't care, and she thinks that she has every right to go through my things. Maybe she simply thinks that they're *our* things.

Figuring that I should just get some sleep and try to sort things out in the morning, I get back into bed. Sleep feels a long way off, however, and I end up simply staring up at the ceiling and listening to the occasional sounds of the other me getting on with things in the front room.

CHAPTER FOURTEEN

"I WAS GOING TO go out into the forest and look for blueberries," I say as I wander through in the morning, with a bowl of cereal in my hands, "but -"

Stopping suddenly, I'm surprised to see the other me sitting at my desk. She has a pencil in her right hand, and she's adding some detail to one of the drawings I've been preparing for a client.

"Oh," she says, looking a little surprised to see me, "I'm sorry, I shouldn't have touched this."

She drops the pencil and gets to her feet.

"It's just," she continues, "while you were in the shower, I noticed this sketch, and I could see you'd been changing one of the sections several times. I'm sure you already figured it out, but I noticed that the level problem could be solved by changing that lower section around." She points at the spot that she's been altering. "See?"

I head over and take a look, and I immediately see that she's right. I've been worrying about that particular detail for so long, yet now it's clear that I completely overlooked a very obvious solution. It's strange how the human mind works sometimes, but as I turn to the other me I can't help but notice that she looks a little pleased with herself, although her faint smile quickly fades away.

"I'm sorry," she says again, before reaching for one of the erasers. "I can undo it."

"No, it's fine," I tell her. "I think you just saved me several more hours of banging my head against the wall."

"It just jumped out at me," she counters. "I know it's your work, I know it's your life and everything, but I saw the problem and the solution and..."

Her voice trails off.

"Sorry," she mutters yet again, before turning and limping back over toward the sofa, which she's already tidied and put back to its usual state. "I won't do it again," she adds. "I guess it's just been strange over the past six months, not having any work to do. I get kind of restless."

"I know the feeling," I reply.

"My foot feels a lot better," she adds. "I don't want to inconvenience you anymore."

"You can't go back out to live in the forest

again," I tell her. "It's crazy."

"I don't want to get in your way."

"You're not," I say with a sigh, before realizing that I could perhaps sound a little more enthusiastic. "Listen, I have room here. And it's not like we're exactly different people. I'd rather you stayed than went back out into the forest."

She turns to me, and I can see that she's a little troubled.

"Just make sure to let me know if I over-step any boundaries," she says cautiously. "It's weird being here. Please let me know if I seem to be forgetting that I'm just a guest. After all, I'm not from this world. I'm the *other* Ann, the one who came here and kind of threw you for a loop." She pauses. "I just want you to know that I understand my place," she adds finally. "I'm not trying to be someone or something I'm not."

"I never thought that you were," I reply. "And thank you, honestly. You really helped me out with that sketch."

She smiles.

***

"Hey, cut it out," I mutter as I feel Sheba once again brushing against my legs. "I'm trying to work."

It's late afternoon, and I've been getting on with the sketches all day. The other me limped outside after lunch, saying that she wanted to take a look around, so I've been able to work in relative peace. Now, however, Sheba seems to have stirred from her nap on the bed, and she's trying desperately to get my attention. It's not feeding time, so I'm not sure exactly why she's bugging me, but I guess maybe she's still not quite sure what's going on in the house. After all, the other me must seem very confusing.

"I just need to do a little more and then I'm with you," I tell her. "Seriously, Sheba, Mommy has to pay for your food and treats somehow. Go nap for a while and I'll fetch you when I'm ready to play."

She meows, and I look down to see her staring up at me.

"What?" I ask, feeling a little exasperated now.

I wait, but she simply continues to look up at me with that same inscrutable expression. She obviously wants *something*, but it can't be food and I doubt she thinks that it's playtime.

"What?" I ask again. "I'm not a mind-reader."

She begins to meow again, but suddenly we both hear a banging sound. Turning, I see the other me limping up the porch steps, and then I look back down just in time to see Sheba bolting away, racing between the chairs and then disappearing quickly into my bedroom.

I guess I was right. She *is* finding this hard.

"Can I disturb you for a moment?"

I turn to see the other me standing at the open back door.

"Sorry," she continues, "but I need to get your opinion on something. I've been busy outside, but I don't want to get too far with things until I've got your permission."

"Sure," I reply, setting my pencil down before getting to my feet and heading over to the door. "I was starting to wonder what you'd been doing out there for so long. And I was thinking of going for a jog soon, so I don't mind taking a break."

"I used to love jogging," she says. "Maybe when my ankle's fully healed, I'll come with you."

"Sure," I reply. "Why not?"

"It's a little project based on something I did back in my own world," she says, as she leads me down the steps and around to the side of the house. "I noticed you didn't seem to have done anything similar, but that makes sense. I mean, I only did it after things starting going wrong with the world, and obviously you haven't had to deal with anything like that. It's completely natural that you wouldn't have done something like this when everything here is so perfect."

"This world has its moments too," I mutter.

"Ta-da!"

She stops ahead of me, and I'm startled to see that she's rigged up some kind of water-collecting system that seems to be fed by the gutter. I've been meaning to fix the gutter for a while, but I never quite got around to the job. Now, however, the other me has clearly used items from the basement to set up what looks like a very complex system that collects water from various spots on the roof and channels it into a large plastic barrel that's been sitting around unused. Frankly, this is far superior to anything that I had in mind.

"Before you ask," she says, "I have a way to keep it clean, and to sterilize it once it's been collected. I used this exact set-up back in my world, and it worked perfectly."

Feeling somewhat speechless, I stare at the contraption.

"I can take it down," she adds. "I didn't mean to bug you earlier, but I can have this undone by evening if you want. I just thought I could help."

"No, it's great," I tell her. "It's... more than great. I was planning on doing something similar one summer, but I always ended up getting side-tracked. There just never seems to be enough time in the day to get on with projects like this." I pause, still admiring her work, before turning and seeing that she's smiling, as if she's really proud. After a moment, I notice that there are tears in her eyes.

"Are you okay?" I ask.

"I'm fine," he replies, sniffing the tears back. "Sorry, it's just that when I think about how this house looked when I left it in my world, and when I look at it now."

She turns and looks up at her water system, and I spot a tear trickling down her cheek.

"This is a really good addition to the house," I say, following her gaze and admiring her work. "Thank you."

CHAPTER FIFTEEN

Six days later...

"THEN I CLEARED AN area just beyond the treeline," the other me explains breathlessly, as we sit with Donna at the dining room table, "and I prepared it for use later in the season. We've been discussing our plans, and I'm going to be basically setting up a series of planting areas for different crops. I'm going to start with garlic and onions and some herbs, and then progress to some more ambitious ideas. I also want to build some raised beds that I can use next summer, but I'm going to wait to do that until after I've finished building this drainage system that I think will really improve the soil. We're going to be pretty self-sufficient before too long."

"It's true," I say to Donna, managing to get a rare word in. "We are."

"You two have been busy," Donna replies.

"It's really not much to do with me," I tell her. "It's the other..."

I turn to the other me.

"It's Ann's work," I add, suddenly worrying about how to refer to her. "The other... I guess you know what I mean."

"It's so much easier doing this when you have a long-term plan," the other me says, apparently unfazed as she turns back to Donna. "Back in my old world, I was just trying to find a way to survive. Here, I can access information online and I can really go to town. I mean, I can go to town figuratively, and I can also go to town literally. We're planning a trip to a garden center."

"I wanted to check about that," I say to Donna. "We're okay to travel a short distance, right?"

"Of course," she replies. "No-one wants you to be prisoners here. In fact, seeing as the pair of you are getting on so well, I guess this is a good time to let you know that we're changing the schedule for my visits. I won't lie to you, funding problems are a part of this, but there's also the fact that I can see how well you're doing. So instead of coming every Thursday, I'm going to start coming once a month, on the first."

"Once a month?" I say, shocked by the suggestion. "Not more?"

"Do you think I *need* to come more?" she asks.

"I..."

Turning to the other me, I can see that she looks apprehensive, as if she's worried about how I'm going to answer.

"No," I say finally, turning back to Donna, "absolutely not. I'm just surprised that *you're* okay with that."

"I can't help thinking back to the day I first brought you two together," she replies with a smile. "I had faith, though. I knew you could overcome any problems, and now look at you. You're like two peas in a pod. I don't mind admitting that I'm going to start using your case as an example in training programs. You two are honestly the most successful integration I've been involved with so far. I have no doubt that once a month will be fine, but remember that you can call me at any time and I'll come sooner. That goes for both of you."

I turn to the other me again, and she looks really pleased with this development.

"You two are a dream team," Donna continues, as I turn back to see her beaming at me. "This is one for the record books. You two are like *The Odd Couple* right now!"

***

"So once a month is really going to be okay?" I ask as I follow Donna across the yard, heading toward her car. "Because I don't mind, say, every two weeks or something like that."

"Once a month is fine," she replies. "Stop worrying."

"But you mentioned budget cuts," I continue, my mind whirring with all the possibilities. "Are you sure you're not just cutting your visits because you have to hit some kind of target?"

"Ann..."

"I just think that this seems really quick," I stammer. "It's been three weeks since she arrived and since you were making all these heavy pronouncements about how hard this'll be, and now suddenly you think we can go for a whole month without any help."

She turns to me, but in my haste I bump into her with enough force to dislodge her files and folders. Her paperwork spills out all across the ground.

"Sorry," I add, immediately crouching down to gather everything back up. I know I must seem like a paranoid mess, but I can't help myself. "I just feel like this is moving very fast now. *Too* fast."

"Leave all this, I'll pick it up," she replies as

she bends over to grab the papers. "And stop fussing, Ann. You have my number, and my e-mail. You can contact me at any time, and I'm only a few hours' drive away."

"I know," I tell her, "but it just seems as if -"

Suddenly I freeze as I see a photo of the other me, attached to the front of a file bearing the title 'Emergency Psychiatric Analysis Results' and the emblem of somewhere called the Cottonhurst Psychiatric Facility. I look down to the bottom of the page and spot a name, Doctor Anton Mellor, and then the papers are pulled from my hands.

"Stop worrying," Donna says firmly. "Get on with your life. That approach seems to have been working out so far."

"What's Cottonhurst Psychiatric Facility?" I ask, as she picks up the last of the papers. "Was the other me sent to some kind of institution?"

She sighs.

I glance back at the house, but there's no sign of the other Ann so I get to my feet.

"I deserve to know," I continue, lowering my voice a little. "Why was she assessed by someone at a psychiatric hospital? Is that standard for all the people who came to our world, or did something happen?"

"Ann -"

"Because I've read a lot about the processes, and I never heard about psychiatric assessments being carried out en masse."

"The other Ann is absolutely fine," she says firmly.

"And she's got the certificate to prove it?"

"The mental and emotional well-being of all the visitors is our priority. I've been very open with you already, most of the visitors have been through very difficult situations. We gave them support where necessary, and we only cleared them for release once we were absolutely certain that there won't be any problems." She places a hand on my shoulder. "You have to trust me. Would I switch to monthly visits if I had even the slightest inkling of a worry?"

"What's in her file?" I ask.

"You know I can't tell you."

"Why not?"

"I can't share one client's personal information with another."

"She's me!" I hiss.

"I'll see you in a month," she replies, as she opens her car door and climbs inside, "and you can call me in a week or two, if you like, to let me know how things are going. Now stop fussing and start focusing on how well things have been going. You two have already done so brilliantly. I honestly can't wait to see how you're doing next time I come visit."

With that, she starts the car and reverses it

across the yard, before driving away along the road that twists and turns through the forest.

After a moment, I turn and look back toward the house.

CHAPTER SIXTEEN

AS SOON AS I reach the front door, I realize I can hear the TV running inside the house. That in itself is a little unusual, since neither myself or the other Ann watch TV a lot, but as I step inside I realize to my surprise that she's not just watching any old show. She's watching *Doppelgangers Gone Bad*.

"Despite calling her case worker nine times over the course of a week," the voice-over intones sternly, "Jenny Rivers was never offered any help. As her fears grew, she began to keep a diary of her doppelganger's behavior, a diary she soon began to share with one of her neighbors. Sadly for Jenny, this final attempt to get help came far too late."

The screen shows a burning house at night, with firefighters struggling desperately to deal with the blaze.

I step forward, but the other Ann has her eyes glued to the screen and she doesn't seem to have noticed that I'm here.

"When Jenny's body was pulled from the ashes," the voice-over continues, "it was assumed that the fire had been the cause of death. A few days later, however, an autopsy revealed that she'd suffered from thirty-six stab wounds, more than half of which were in her face. Investigators said that she'd been subjected to one of the most frenzied attacks they'd ever encountered."

Suddenly the other Ann turns to me, and she stares for a moment before finally managing to smile.

"Sound off," she stammers, and the image is muted.

"Hey," I reply. "How are things going in here?"

"Sorry," she says, getting to her feet. "When Donna mentioned *The Odd Couple*, I got to thinking that I'd like to see an episode again." She pauses. "Then, when I turned the TV on, it started to auto-play this show about doubles murdering their hosts in this world."

"Huh," I say, forcing a smile of my own. "Random, huh?"

"It said you had the entire series queued," she replies. "You're onto something like episode two hundred."

"Fancy that," I say, trying to play the whole thing off. "You know, I think I might have stumbled across that show a long time ago. It's just reality trash, right? There's no point having it on."

She stares at me, before turning to look back at the screen, where there's now an image of a field, with a figure in the distance running frantically. A moment later, police helicopters swoop into view and the camera zooms in to reveal a terrified-looking woman yelling at the cops.

"You might as well turn this off," I say, as I realize that this must be Jenny Rivers' doppelganger getting apprehended for murder. "It's just depressing. And they totally sensationalize things. They take rare, horrible events and make them seem like they're happening all the time, when everyone knows that really the world is much safer."

The view on the screen wobbles for a moment, and then suddenly shots ring out and the woman drops dead to the ground with a chunk of her head missing. Police officers start rushing toward her, and the camera zooms in even further, finally revealing the dead woman's face. Filled with the sudden thought that this is unhealthy, I watch for a moment longer before deciding that I've definitely had enough.

"TV off," I say out loud, and the screen goes dark.

The other Ann stares at the blankness for a

moment, before slowly turning to me.

"Sorry," she mutters finally, shaking her head as if she's emerging from some kind of foggy state, "you're right, there's no need to watch that junk. It's just depressing."

***

While the other Ann is outside, working on some adjustments to her water collection system, I sit at the desk and type the name Cottonhurst Psychiatric Facility into a search engine.

The first thing I find is a press release, issued by the facility itself, announcing that it has won a major contract to help with the implementation of the Rutherford Act. The whole thing is gushing and overwhelmingly positive, but toward the bottom of the page I find a few scraps of detail. Cottonhurst seems to be part of a huge conglomerate that won a lucrative government deal to help integrate the people who came through the portal. The idea is that all the so-called doppelgangers are assessed and – where necessary – they're given help and support to deal with their arrival in this world. There's mention of PTSD and other stresses that might have been caused by the war that broke out in their world.

So far, so good.

I click back and check some other results.

Scrolling down, I find references to Cottonhurst and its parent company having apparently helped lots of people. There are flowery testimonials from people who claim that Cottonhurst and its staff basically saved their lives. I find a few mildly critical comments on some of the articles, but certainly nothing that raises any alarms. Despite my natural skepticism, then, I have to admit that so far Cottonhurst seems to be doing a good job.

I scroll through a few more pages, still finding nothing that seems odd. And then, just as I'm about to try something else, I notice a label at the bottom, mentioning some results having been removed due to court action.

Intrigued, I try to find some information about this court action, but there's nothing.

I glance out the window, and I listen for a moment to the sound of the other me getting on with her work round the other side of the house.

Turning back to the screen, I decide to try a new approach, so I type in the name of the doctor who was mentioned on the other me's file. As soon as I do that, I find that I get almost no results at all. There are a few pages about his career, but at the bottom of the page there's another note about information having been removed. Someone seems to have really tried hard to scrub all information about this guy from the internet. I consider myself to be pretty good at tracking down information, but

I can find absolutely nothing that suggests what happened. Even the court case itself is impossible to locate, suggesting that some kind of pretty tight seal was placed on the situation. Someone definitely wants to keep all mention of this Anton Mellor guy out of the news.

Determined to uncover something, I try searching social media sites.

Every few minutes, I look over my shoulder, just to make absolutely certain that the other me isn't about to come back inside.

I try the obvious sites, and I don't come up with anything, so I start checking the sites that aren't so obvious. Eventually I end up on various foreign-language sites, and finally – after digging for so long that I'm starting to give up hope – I stumble onto a mention of Doctor Mellor on a Chinese social site that I've never even heard of before.

I have to copy and paste the text into a translator, but at least this gives me a garbled version of the story. And as I read, I start to realize that this Mellor guy definitely seems to have been at the heart of something pretty bad. The translation's pretty poor, but I keep coming across words like 'suspended' and 'scandal'. It's evident that Doctor Mellor did something bad, and the gist of the article seems to be that he failed to properly diagnose problems with some of the patients he handled.

And then I spot a name that I recognize.

Michael Wallace.

I tell myself that this can't be the same Michael Wallace who was featured in an episode of *Doppelgangers Gone Bad*, but I soon discover that it is the same man after all. Doctor Mellor seems to have dealt with his doppelganger and passed him fit for integration. The TV show went into great detail about how badly the integration went, although after a moment I can't help but wonder why the show never mentioned Doctor Mellor. I can only assume that even the show's producers didn't want to risk incurring the wrath of Cottonhurst and its parent company. The fear effect must have been pretty strong.

At the end of the article, there's mention of suicide, and it's quite clear that Doctor Mellor killed himself at some point. After which, his employers apparently went to extreme lengths to make sure that word about his activities never leaked out.

But if the other me was one of his patients, and if there's any chance that something bad happened at Cottonhurst, then Donna should have been completely honest with me.

CHAPTER SEVENTEEN

"HEY," I SAY AS I wander around the side of the house and find the other me perched up on the roof, working on the guttering. "I'm going to go for a jog before the bad weather sets in. Looks like there's more rain on the way."

"Okay," she replies, sounding a little breathless as she turns to me and smiles. "If you wait half an hour, I could change and come with you."

"It's not going to be a long one," I tell her, "and I really *am* worried about the weather. We can go some other time."

"Sure. That's fine by me."

She turns and gets back to work, and it looks as if she's trying to force one section of guttering into another. I watch for a moment, fully aware that

I should get going and leave her alone, but at the same time I can't help thinking about the stuff I read online today. I'm itching to find out whether the other me reacts to any mention of the names Cottonhurst or Anton Mellor, but at the same time I don't want to blunder into something that I'm not prepared for. I really should think about this some more, and maybe call Donna some time and demand to be told the truth.

Or am I just being paranoid?

"Are you okay?" the other me asks after a moment, and it's clear that she realizes I'm staring at her.

"I'm fine," I reply, taking a step back and forcing a smile. "Sorry, you know what it's like. Starting a run is always the hard part."

"I remember," she says, before taking a hammer and starting to bang on the side of the gutter. "I'm exactly the same."

***

The path dips from its crest and runs down steeply toward the lake road. I'm running a little faster than usual, and I never have music when I'm jogging so the only sound is a constant thud-thud-thud from my feet as I race along. I'd usually have taken a break at the old crossroads, but today I powered on through. Finally, however, I come to a halt at a bench overlooking the lake, and I try to get my breath back as I look out across the glittering, sun-dappled water.

For a moment, everything seems absolutely perfect.

Suddenly hearing a rustling sound, I turn and look over my shoulder. I watch the path, expecting to see some hiker or rambler wandering into view, but there's no sign of anyone. It's rare to bump into anyone else out here, but not completely impossible. I watch for a moment longer, and then I turn and start walking for a few paces.

I'm still a little out of breath from my run, but I'm starting to think that instead of turning back I might go for what I call a 'mega run', which means heading east for a few more miles before circling back along the ancient highway that leads eventually to a road that runs past my place. I'd been planning just a short jog, but the weather seems to be holding up and somehow I feel like being out of the house for a while longer. Besides, if I get wet, that's not the absolute worst thing.

Just as I'm about to start running again, however, I hear the same rustling sound as before, only closer. I turn and look along the path again, and this time I can't help but feel a little worried. I can sense someone watching me, although I quickly tell myself that I must be imagining things. Usually when I come out here, I experience a blissful state of being all alone, but this time I swear it's as if someone's nearby. I look around, still telling myself to get a grip, but the sensation continues.

I almost call out, but at the last moment I stop myself.

Calling out would be dumb.

Calling out would just fuel the idiocy.

So I turn and set off again, running along the path, and I soon forget all my earlier concerns. I feel energized, as if I'm in the form of my life, and now I'm determined to have a 'mega run'. As long as I'm back before dark, that's all that matters. I feel really free as I get closer to the lake, and finally I stop again as I reach a little outcrop overlooking the shore.

For a moment, I have to bend over and rest with my hands against my knees as I struggle to get my breath back, but then I step forward and look out across the lake. I use a hand to shield my eyes from the sun, and for a few seconds I'm utterly mesmerized by the beauty of the light as it catches little ripples on the water.

I'm so lucky to live out here.

Turning, I'm about to set off again, when I suddenly hear another rustling sound, this time coming from just over my shoulder. I begin to turn, but immediately something slams straight into my back. Startled, I stumble forward, and I'm too late to catch my balance.

Crying out, I fall over the edge of the outcrop and tumble down until I slam hard into the ground far below.

CHAPTER EIGHTEEN

WHEN I OPEN MY eyes, everything is dark.

I blink, and for a moment I don't know where I am or how I got here. I wait for everything to come rushing back, but instead I feel as if there's a hole in my mind. This is like the very few times I ever got drunk, except that I know I haven't been drinking. I wait a moment longer, just in case the memories return, and then I try to sit up.

Gasping as a sharp pain runs up my right arm, I roll onto my back and see a familiar shape high above, and I realize that I'm in my bed. I stare at the light fitting for a moment, as I try to remember how I got here, and then I hear footsteps coming closer from somewhere in the house.

"Are you awake?" the other Ann asks, and suddenly she leans over me. She looks worried.

"Can you hear me? Say something."

"What happened?" I ask, still trying to break through the block in my mind.

"Do you know your name?"

"What?"

"Tell me your name."

"Ann. Why are you asking me that?"

"When's your birthday?"

"July the seventh, but -"

"Who's the current President of the United States of America?"

"What?"

"Just answer."

"Butler," I reply. "Chance Butler."

She lets out a relieved sigh.

"Okay," she says finally, "that's good. Those were the three questions the book said to ask when you woke up. Do you have a headache?"

"No. Why? What's going on?"

"Nausea?"

"No. Tell me what's happening!"

"That's good," she replies, "I don't think you're concussed. You're lucky."

"I don't understand any of this," I say, before trying once again to sit up. Again, however, I feel a sharp pain in my arm, and I have to really struggle for a moment before finally I manage to sit on the side of the bed. As soon as I try to put any weight on my right foot, however, I feel a burst of pain.

"Careful!" the other me says, kneeling next to me. "What do you remember? How did you fall?"

"Fall?"

I'm about to ask what she means, but then I remember being out on my run. I was watching the lake, and then I felt something slam into me from behind, and then I fell.

And then?

"I think you got mugged," the other me explains. "I know it sounds crazy, but hear me out. When I found you, your purse and phone were missing. You *did* take those with you, didn't you?"

"I did," I reply, "but what do you mean? You *found* me?"

"I was so worried when you didn't come back from your jog," she tells me. "By the time it got dark, I was seriously freaking out. I didn't want to go crazy and call the police, so I took a flashlight and headed out along the path I used to take when I went jogging. I figured you'd probably gone the same way. I used to sometimes go on what I called a 'mega run', but I always made sure to be back before dark."

"Someone hit me," I whisper, replaying that moment over and over in my mind. "Someone pushed me."

"I almost went right past you," she continues. "I was calling your name. It was dark, it was the middle of the night. And then, by some miracle, I happened to spot you down there near the side of the lake. I probably shouldn't tell you this, but when I saw you at first, I was terrified that you were..."

Her voice trails off.

"Anyway," she says after a moment, "I managed to carry you back here. I tried calling for help, but your phone was missing and there's no landline, and the internet's not working, so I didn't know what to do. You've been in bed all day, but I was starting to think I might have to take the bike and cycle to the nearest town for help." She reaches out and touches the side of my face. "I'm so glad you're awake."

"What's up with my ankle?" I ask. "And my arm?"

"I don't know. Hopefully they're not broken, only sprained or something. I think you'd be in much more pain if they were broken."

I try again to put weight on my damaged foot, but the pain is strong enough to make me quickly stop.

"I think you should just rest for a while," the other me says. "Give it a day or two, and I'm sure you'll be fine again, but only if you give your body time to heal. Don't worry, I'll look after you. Good job I'm here, huh?"

"I need to call the police," I tell her.

"Someone tried to kill me."

"Like I said, we don't have a phone and the internet's down."

"Have you tried resetting the router?"

"I've tried everything. I don't know about this world, but where I come from, it's not uncommon to go a few days at a time without being able to contact the outside world. Even the TV doesn't work."

I pause for a moment as I try to figure out what I should do next. The other me is probably right about the importance of rest, and I guess I can't go hopping around the place. At the same time, I feel as if I can't just sit here placidly after everything that has happened. Someone actually robbed me out there on the path! Someone left me for dead!

"Are you hungry?" the other me asks. "I made soup."

Turning to her, I can't help thinking that she's looking at me strangely. I swear, there's almost a smile on her lips.

"I'll get you some soup," she says, suddenly getting to her feet and heading toward the door. "I baked some bread, too. I know it sounds odd, but I had to keep myself busy while you were unconscious. I was pretty much going crazy for a while." She stops and turns to me. "You know, when I was carrying you back here, I realized it was a little like that time *you* carried *me* back. It's like our roles were reversed. Weird, huh?"

She smiles, and then she whistles as she steps out of view and heads through to the kitchen.

I sit completely still for a moment, trying to process everything that has happened, and then I try yet again to stand up. I instantly have to sit back down, however, as a burst of pain shoots through my damaged ankle. I feel completely helpless, but I quickly tell myself that everything's going to be okay. The internet'll be back up soon, probably within an hour or two, and then I can call to report what happened. I also need to see a doctor. Besides, even if we were completely isolated out here, I'd only have to wait until Donna's next visit in six days' time.

No, wait.

A month.

Donna's not coming for a month, and I have no food deliveries scheduled before then either.

For a few seconds, I feel a sense of panic starting to rise through my chest, but then I tell myself to stop worrying so much. I'll be up and about in no time, and everything will get back to normal. I just need to stay calm.

CHAPTER NINETEEN

"THAT FREEZER IN YOUR back room is immense," the other me says the following morning, as she brings a bowl of cereal through for me. "I mean, I was the same in my world, I had deliveries once a month. But it looks like you stock up for three or four months at a time."

"Have you tried the internet again?" I ask.

"Still nothing."

"Can you bring my laptop through?"

"Oh, sure, I forgot. Sorry. I'll bring it next time I come in."

She sets the bowl on the nightstand next to my bed.

"Don't worry," she continues, "I'm on it. I mean, I'm on everything. You don't have to worry that things are going to go to pot while you're recuperating, because I have everything taken care of. Even that weird cat of yours. I'll be honest, the cat is the only real difference between your world and mine. I never had a cat like Sheba. These little differences are pretty weird, aren't they?"

"Thanks for the cereal," I reply, "but would you mind grabbing my laptop for me? I really want to check something."

"Sure, just give me a moment." She sits on the edge of the bed. "Sheba's so picky, isn't she? She won't eat any food that falls outside her bowl, not even if you pick it up and put it back in for her. Another thing I've noticed is that even though she's still not sure about me, she's started to come a little closer sometimes. It's as if she -"

"Sorry," I say, interrupting her, "but I really need to do something on my laptop. I'm going nuts here, just doing nothing. I think I might take a look at some notes I was making about the Henry project."

"Oh, I made a few changes to that already."

"I'm sorry?"

"Shouldn't I have done that?" She stares at me for a moment. "I'm really sorry if I overstepped the mark. It's just that, while I was trying to sort out the internet, I saw the files on your laptop. I think I figured out how to make the gazebo work. It was one of those things that seems obvious once you notice it, but..." Her voice trails off for a moment.

"I've invaded your privacy," she adds finally. "I'm so sorry."

"No, it's fine," I tell her. I mean, sure, I feel a little irritated, but I guess there's no need for that. "Thank you."

She stares at me for a moment, but I'm not entirely sure what she's waiting for.

"Okay," she says suddenly, getting to her feet, "I'll get that laptop for you, and then I was thinking I should probably help you shower. So I'll get that going and then I'll leave you alone to do some work. Deal?"

***

"There you go," she says a short while later, as she helps me ease down onto a chair that she's placed in the shower cubicle. "Don't worry, the water's already nice and warm. I'll be back in a moment to help you."

She reaches up and turns the shower head, sending pleasantly warm water crashing down onto my naked body.

"It's okay," I tell her, "I can do the rest myself."

"Are you sure?"

I turn to reach out for the various bottles on the floor, but then I gasp as I feel another rush of pain in my right arm. I wiggle my fingers successfully, but that's about the limit of my abilities.

"I think I might have fractured something," I say.

"I'll help you," she replies, heading out of the bathroom and through into the hallway. "Just wait a moment."

Once she's gone, I try again to reach for the bottles, but again I find that I can't quite manage. I hate being this helpless. I've never relied on another person, not since I was a kid. Not like this. Yet here I am, not even able to wash myself properly. I know I should probably just relax and accept the situation, but at the same time I feel as if I'm about to scream with impotent rage. Closing my eyes, I take a series of deep breaths and try to stay calm.

"Okay, here we go," the other me says, and I open my eyes just as she comes back through and steps into the cubicle.

She's completely naked.

"What are you doing?" I ask.

"Helping you in the shower." She picks up one of the bottles. "What's wrong?"

I stare at her, but for a moment I'm completely speechless.

"It makes sense for me to shower at the same time," she continues, with a faint, nervous smile on her face. "Is that a problem?"

"No," I lie, although I feel distinctly

uncomfortable.

"It's not like there's anything either of us hasn't seen before," she points out.

I'm about to reply and tell her again that it's fine, but at that moment I see that she has quite a lot of scars on her body. Particularly around her lower abdomen and down onto her legs, she has thick lines that have been cut into her flesh, with scores of these lines criss-crossing her body. I swallow hard as I realize that perhaps there's still a lot that I don't know about her experiences before she came to this world.

"They're from the war," she says, as she kneels in front of me and pours some shower gel into the palm of her hand. "I haven't told you everything. I didn't want to upset you."

"Right," I reply weakly, not really knowing what to say. "I get it. You don't want to talk about it."

"It's not really that," she says, before reaching out and starting to rub the gel across my shoulders. "It's more that I don't want to put you through it. I mean, there were times when I thought I was really about to die, when I got cut up really badly. People do things when they're desperate. People did things to me, and then – in order to survive – I sometimes had to do things to them in return. To defend myself. To escape."

I nod as she puts more gel on her hands, and

then suddenly she reaches out and starts washing my chest and belly. I flinch slightly at the feel of her hands on my bare skin, but I try to hide my discomfort.

"Apart from the scars, though," he continues, "our bodies are basically the same, aren't they? They don't really look very different. You even have the same moles and freckles that I have."

"I guess that's only natural," I reply.

She grabs a sponge and starts washing my legs. After a moment she gently pushes my legs apart, and I let her. Even though everything about this situation feels wrong, I know I have to stay polite, and the last thing I want is to offend her. She's helping me out, and I'm the one who seems to be finding this whole thing unusual. Not her. I'm the one who needs to do better.

"I've come to term with the scars now," she explains, as she continues to clean me. "It took a while, but I figure it's not as if I can get rid of them. They're a reminder of what I went through, but also of the fact that I survived. A lot of people didn't."

"I know," I say, and then she looks up at me and smiles.

I wait for her to say something, but now she's simply staring at me as the water continues to crash down all around us. I want to break the awkward silence, but I'm really not sure how, and then after a moment she leans a little closer. Again, I feel as if I should say something, yet I can't think of a single thing that wouldn't sound trite and stupid. I guess I just need to accept the silence.

Then, suddenly, she leans even closer and kisses me.

For a moment – maybe three or four seconds – I let her. As our lips touch, I feel her tongue slipping into my mouth, and I don't push her away. The kiss feels wrong and unnatural somehow, but it's also the first time that I've been kissed by anyone in many, many years, and I can't deny that on some level it also feels good.

And then, just as suddenly, she puts a hand on the side of my waist, and I pull away in shock.

"What?" she asks, looking worried as she fixes me with an intense stare. "I mean... Don't you want to see what it'd be like?"

"I..."

For a moment, I consider letting her kiss me again. The whole idea is insane, but – for a fraction of a second – my mind's eye is filled with an image of what might happen if I let her continue. It all feels so wrong, but also very right, and it takes a couple of seconds before I realize that I have to stop this right now.

"I don't think it's a good idea," I say cautiously. "I think it'd just be way too weird."

She stares at me, and then she smiles and puts some shower gel onto the sponge.

"You're right," she says. "I'm sorry, I don't know what came over me. Please, just forget it ever happened. I hope this won't make things weird between us."

CHAPTER TWENTY

CAREFULLY, AND VERY SLOWLY, I lower my right foot onto the carpet next to my bed, and I begin to press down. I feel an immediate sliver of pain, of course, but not as much as before. It's late afternoon, and I've been resting all day in bed and working on some notes, and now I think my ankle has actually begun to feel a little better. Not enough to walk on it just yet, of course, but at least it's a sign of progress.

"Are you okay in here?" the other me asks, and I turn to see her coming into the room.

I wish she'd knock.

"You're not trying to walk, are you?" she adds.

"Just testing," I reply, "to see how things are going." I press again, and this time I'm more prepared for the pain. More able to push through. "I think I'll be up and about soon. No more lolling around in bed. I don't think I can take another day like today."

"You really shouldn't stress yourself too much," she says, and she seems a little worried by the prospect of me becoming more mobile again. "Better to be safe than sorry."

"The pain's already going down a little," I tell her, as I gently put some more pressure on my foot. "I think I'll be okay in the morning." I take a moment to tease my foot a little, pressing several times and then releasing for a few seconds.

After a moment, I glance at the other me and see that she's watching my foot intently. Her brow is slightly furrowed, and I still can't shake the feeling that she's unhappy with the fact that I'm not in more pain. Then again, I know that can't be true, so I focus on trying to ease my damaged ankle back into use. In all honesty, the pain is getting a little worse, but I don't want to admit that just yet. I want to look stronger.

"Wait!" the other me says suddenly, getting to her feet and hurrying to the door. "I've got an idea!"

I open my mouth to call after her, but she's already out of the room. I have no idea where she's gone, but I don't mind being alone for a while. I wince slightly as I try again to put pressure on my damaged foot, and this time I decide to see whether I can actually stand. I knew there'll be pain, but I'm determined to prove – if only to myself – that I can do this. I take a deep breath, gently bite my bottom lip, and finally I start getting to my feet.

I immediately let out a gasp of pain, but then I manage to switch most of the pressure onto my undamaged ankle.

"Hey!"

The other me hurries back through, and I'm surprised to see that she's brought one of the old fence posts that I stored in the shed a few years ago.

"I was thinking you might be able to use this as a crutch!" she says. "Be careful. Try it."

"I think I might be okay," I reply cautiously.

"No, you have to use the crutch!"

Before I can reply, she pushes the post against me.

"Just wait a moment," I stammer, annoyed that she's starting to crowd me just as I'm managing to wobble unaided. "I can do this!"

"No, you need to support yourself!"

"I'm already -"

Suddenly the fence post slams down against my damaged ankle, and I scream as I try to pull away. Stumbling, I lose my balance and fall. I reach out to grab the bed, but I'm too late and I thud down against the carpet. As I do so, my damaged foot hits the bottom of the nightstand and I cry out again.

"I told you to be careful!" the other me gasps, dropping to her knees and trying to help me up.

"Leave me alone!" I snap.

"You're pushing yourself too hard, you -"

"Leave me alone!" I yell, pushing her away with such force that she falls back and bumps against the wall. "I keep telling you! Why won't you just leave me alone and let me get on with it!"

"I was only -"

"I told you to stop!" I hiss, as I wait for the pain in my ankle to subside. "Why did you have to keep pushing like that? I kept telling you to stop!"

"I'm sorry!" she sobs.

"You rammed that damn thing straight into my ankle!"

"No! I didn't, I swear!"

"You did! You did it on purpose!"

She stares at me, her expression filled with shock, and then she stumbles to her feet and runs out of the room.

"I didn't mean it like that!" I shout, but it's too late and I can already hear her head out into the yard. Sighing, I turn and look at my ankle, and already the pain is starting to really throb. "Damn it! It's worse than ever!"

CHAPTER TWENTY-ONE

STOPPING IN THE DOORWAY, I take a moment to listen to the quietness of the house. I heard the other me come back a few minutes ago, after being out all afternoon, but she hasn't come through to check on me. After a few seconds I hear a faint bumping sound coming from the front room, followed by the creak of the sofa.

Leaning on the wooden post, which is actually working pretty well as a crutch now, I limp out into the hallway and over to the door at the far end, and then I stop as soon as I see the other me sitting on the sofa as she reads a book.

Sheba is next to her on the sofa, purring happily as she's stroked.

For a moment, I can only stare at the bizarre scene. The other me is wearing my clothes, which is fine since I told her to take anything she wanted from my wardrobe. She also seems to have changed her hair slightly, making it look pretty much identical to mine, and I can't shake the sensation that I'm basically watching myself. I can't even see her scars from here.

It's like looking into a mirror, except that the image isn't even reversed.

Suddenly she turns to me, but she doesn't seem very surprised. I guess she heard me coming through from the bedroom.

"Hey," I say cautiously, wondering how I'm going to start my apology. "I'm sorry about earlier."

"It's fine," she replies. "You were in pain. I understand."

"No, I was out of order," I tell her, as I lean on the crutch and limp into the room. "You were trying to help me, and I shouldn't have yelled."

"I'd have done exactly the same thing," she says calmly.

"It was wrong of me," I reply. "I know you didn't do it on purpose."

I wait for her to say something, but she simply stares at me as I edge closer.

"Sheba seems to like you," I point out, forcing a smile. "I knew she just had to get used to the idea of there being two of me."

"It's okay," she says. "I'm the other. She senses that I'm different."

"The crutch works really well," I continue. "Thank you so much, I never would have thought to try it."

"Yes, you would," she replies. "Of course you would."

"It doesn't matter how much pain I was in," I tell her, "it was unfair of me to snap like that. I can only hope that you'll forgive me."

"There's nothing to forgive," she replies, as she continues to stroke Sheba. "Like I said, I'd have done exactly the same thing. I appreciate the apology but there's no need. I'm just glad that the crutch works."

"I guess the internet didn't come back, did it?" I ask.

"No."

"I didn't think so." As I reach the sofa, I lean down to give Sheba a pat. "I'm not -"

Suddenly Sheba turns to me and hisses, and before I can react she reaches out and scratches my hand.

"What's *that* about?" I gasp, stepping back and looking down to see a trickle of blood running from my knuckles.

"I'm sure she's just confused," the other me replies, before getting to her feet and heading to the kitchen. "I should go and see what I can rustle up for dinner."

"Thank you," I reply, as I ease myself down

onto the sofa and look at Sheba, who's staring at me with an expression of pure hatred.

I hesitate, before holding my hand out again.

"It's me," I tell her, hoping that I can make her understand. "I know this is pretty confusing, but it's me, sweetheart. The real me, not the other me. You realize that, don't you?"

I reach closer, and she immediately starts hissing again, so I pull back.

"Come on, you know this," I say firmly, keeping my voice low so as to not be overheard. "I raised you from a kitten. I look after you every day. I let you sleep on my bed whenever you want. I know you know that I'm the real me."

I pause, and then I reach out again.

She immediately starts hissing, but I tell myself that I need to push through and force her to understand what's happening here.

"Hey," I continue, "it's -"

Before I can finish, she swipes a paw at me again. I pull away as her claws catch my wrist, and then I watch helplessly as she leaps off the sofa and runs out of the room. I've never seen her look so spooked, not even when the other me turned up, and for a moment I can only sit in stunned silence.

"I wouldn't force it," the other me says as she comes back through and grabs the remote control. She turns the TV on and then comes and sits next to me. "Give her time."

"I thought the TV didn't work," I reply.

"Oh." She pauses, and then she shrugs. "I forgot. Looks like it's working again."

"Then maybe the internet's back!"

"It won't be."

"I need to check."

Raising myself slowly and painfully from the sofa, I take a moment to steady myself on the crutch and then I start limping back through to my room.

"There's no point checking," the other me says calmly. "It was just a coincidence that they both went off at the same time. Just because the TV's back on, that doesn't mean the internet is going to be working."

"It might."

I limp toward the door, but then suddenly I freeze as I hear a familiar voice booming from the TV behind me.

"Tonight, on *Doppelgangers Gone Bad*," the voice-over announces over ominous music, "we look at one of the most horrifying cases to date, and one that flips the table on our usual stories. What motivated thirty-six-year-old Gloria Reeves to kill her own doppelganger? She claims she was only defending herself, but tonight we present exclusive new evidence that paints a very different picture."

Slowly, I turn and look for a moment at the screen, and then I glance over at the other me. She's staring intently at the screen.

"Don't worry," she says calmly, still focused on the screen, "dinner's on. I thought I'd watch some of this while I wait. I know it's cheesy reality stuff, but I guess it might be interesting after all."

I watch the TV for a moment and see gruesome images, and then I turn and head slowly through to my room. Once I'm on the bed, I try the laptop, but of course the internet still doesn't work. What confuses me, however, is the fact that my TV and internet are linked. As I sit on the edge of the bed, I can't quite understand why one would be working while the other remains dead.

CHAPTER TWENTY-TWO

"I WAS THINKING I might go for a jog tomorrow," the other me says later, as we sit eating bolognese at the dining table. "I might try to run all the way around the lake. If it's not raining, obviously."

"That sounds nice," I reply, glad that we seem to be talking about normal, everyday things again. "I think it might be a week or two before I'm able to join you."

"I know. I just think that it can get quite stuffy in here, you know? I'd like to get out and really get some air into my lungs. Don't worry if I'm gone all day, I know my way around. I haven't forgotten."

We sit in silence for a moment.

"I saw you'd been doing some more work in

the yard," I say finally, keen to get the conversation re-started. "It looks like you've taken some of the old tools out of the shed."

"I wanted to see what you had," she replies. "To be honest, it was mostly the same stuff that I had in my shed, back in the real world." She pauses. "I mean, back in *my* world. Sorry, I didn't mean for that to come out the way it sounded."

"No, I understand," I tell her.

"I shouldn't be rude," she says. "I keep reminding myself that I mustn't say things like that around the other me, but sometimes stuff just slips out."

"It's difficult," I reply, as I scoop up another forkful of meat and pasta. "A lot's happened over the past few months. Over the past few weeks, even. And feel free to root around all you want in the shed. I barely even remember what's in there anymore. Plus, I'm sure there are some pretty meaty spiders lurking in there. I'm surprised you dared to go inside."

"I don't mind spiders."

I glance at her.

"You don't?" I ask.

"Never have."

"That's odd," I reply. "I've been terrified of them since I was a kid."

"Huh." She stares at me for a moment. "I guess we have a few differences after all."

Not really knowing what to say, I put the food in my mouth and chew, hoping to use the time to come up with some new topic. As I continue to chew the bolognese, however, I can't help but feel very uninteresting, and I honestly don't think the other me is really in the mood for talking tonight.

Suddenly I feel something sharp slice through my tongue. I lean forward and spit the food out onto the white tablecloth, and I can already taste blood in my mouth. Sure enough, I stare down in horror at the lump of half-chewed bolognese and I see a sharp piece of glass glistening in the meat.

"There's glass in this!" I gasp.

"There is?"

The other me gets to her feet and comes over to take a look. Crouching down, she reaches over and takes the piece of glass out of the food, as I reach into my mouth and feel a nasty cut on the side of my tongue.

"Sheba knocked a bottle over while I was cooking," the other me says, turning the piece of glass around between her fingers, letting my blood get smeared on the tips. "It broke. You might have heard. I thought I'd cleared up all the pieces, but one must have escaped." She turns to me. "I'm so sorry, are you okay? How bad's the damage?"

"It's just the side of my tongue," I reply, as I dab at my lips with a napkin. "It's nothing."

"You're bleeding."

"It's fine." I take a deep breath and force a smile, determined to make sure that this doesn't turn into a disagreement. "Accidents happen, right? And at least I didn't swallow it. If that had happened, and seeing as how we can't call an ambulance, I might have been in real trouble."

"I doubt you'd have swallowed it," she replies.

"I'd still rather not take the risk."

"Of course not." She pauses, before getting to her feet again and suddenly taking the plate away. "I'll bin this and make something else."

"I'm sure it's fine," I tell her.

"We really can't take the risk," she replies, grabbing her own plate before heading toward the door. "If I missed one piece of glass, I might have missed another. Imagine if something had happened to you. I might have ended up on that *Doppelgangers Gone Bad* show." She turns and smiles. "That was a joke, by the way."

"I know," I reply. "Please don't go to any trouble for me, I'm not even that hungry and I barely did anything today. It's no wonder I don't have a big appetite."

"Are you sure? I could fry up some sausages and make mash to go with them."

"Not for me, thanks," I tell her, before glancing at the clock on the wall and seeing that it's almost 10pm. "In fact, I think I might head through to bed soon. I'm not tired, but I want to get back into a proper routine with my sleeping. Today has been pretty crazy."

"Of course," she replies. "I'll make myself a sandwich and then I think I'll read for a while. Just to calm my mind a little before I go to sleep. I hope your tongue stops hurting soon, and again... I'm really sorry for the glass being in there. That was my fault and I'll make sure that it never happens again." She turns and walks out of the room. "Although," she adds, "maybe I should blame Sheba. After all, she's the one who broke the bottle."

"Great," I mutter once she's gone, "now my own cat is trying to kill me."

I sit in silence for a moment, and I can already taste more blood leaking from the cut on my tongue. I take my napkin and use a clean spot to dab at the cut again, but I know there's not really much point. It'll stop bleeding eventually, all by itself.

CHAPTER TWENTY-THREE

STARTLED, I SIT UP in bed and stare into the darkness. My heart is racing. I was dreaming about being back at school, but then suddenly I heard a scream that seemed to come from -

Suddenly I hear it again, and I realize that the other me is crying out in the front room.

Clambering out of bed, I struggle for a moment to balance with the crutches and then I start hobbling toward the door.

"What's wrong?" I call out, as the other me continues to scream. "I'm coming!"

It takes me about a minute to reach the front room, and then I stop and see that the other me is tossing and turning on the sofa bed. The room is dark, but there's enough moonlight for me to see that she's constantly turning one way and then the other, and now I realize that she's muttering to herself as if something's wrong. A moment later she lets out a sudden loud sob, and then she gasps tilts her head back.

"Wake up!" I hiss, hurrying as fast as I can to reach her. "You're dreaming!"

"No, don't touch me!" she gasps, clearly still locked in some kind of nightmare. "Why do you keep doing this to me? Just let me die!"

I reach out to grab her arm and shake her awake.

"Doctor Mellor, please," she snarls, with her eyes squeezed tight shut. "I don't want to do this. I'd rather be dead!"

I hesitate, as I realize that she just mentioned the name that I tried to research the other day. I don't want her to be suffering like this, but for a moment I wait in case she says anything else that might be useful.

"It hurts so much," she whimpers. "It hurts more and more each time. You don't need to do this to me, I already told you I was sorry for what happened. If you're not going to let me go, just put me out of my misery!"

She rolls onto her other side, with enough force to make the entire sofa bed briefly rattle.

"I can't take it anymore!" she cries, and now her whole body is shaking violently. "You're never going to stop, are you? You're as bad as them! I'd rather be back there than going through this!"

Realizing that I can't let this go on any longer, I grab her arm and start to shake her hard.

"Wake up!" I say firmly. "You're dreaming! You have to -"

Before I can finish, she gasps and turns to look at me. Her eyes are wide open, but she seems utterly shocked. Then, just as I'm about to ask whether she's okay, she leaps up from the bed and throws herself against me, knocking me down and then landing on top of me with her hands gripping my throat.

"Stop!" I gasp, trying to push her away but finding that she's too strong. "It's me! You're awake!"

"I won't let you do it again!" she snarls, her eyes filled with fury as she starts squeezing my throat tighter and tighter. "They don't believe me, but they'll have to now! You're a monster!"

"No!" I splutter, but I'm struggling to breathe now. Reaching up, I put my hands against her shoulders and try desperately to push her off. "Stop! It's me, it's Ann! You have to stop!"

Reaching over to the night-stand, she grabs the lamp and rips it away, and then she holds it up as if she means to bring it crashing down against my head. For a moment she's silhouetted above me, holding the lamp up like a rock, as if she's some kind of caveman filled with murderous rage.

"Stop!" I scream. "Ann, please!"

***

"They said I needed to be assessed," she says calmly a short while later, as we sit at the dining room table with the light on above us. "They sent me to Cottonhurst because they said I was demonstrating emotional instability."

"Because of what happened to you before you escaped your world?"

"Because of what caused the scars," she replies. There are tears in her eyes as she stares at me. "I don't want to go into the details. I lied before, it's not just to spare you. It's also because I don't want to go think about it again. Let's just say that it's probably what you're imagining. Toward the end, before we escaped through the portal, everything was chaotic. The crazy part is, I got off light compared to some people. The things I saw, and heard..."

Her voice trails off.

"They were probably right when they said I needed help," she continues finally, nodding a little, "but going to Cottonhurst wasn't good for anyone. That place was run like a prison. Worse, really. And Doctor Mellor was in charge of it all."

I wait for her to go on, but she seems lost in her thoughts. The last thing I want is to start prodding her and potentially causing her to think back to her experiences, so I decide to wait.

"He ran that place like his own little kingdom," she says after a few more seconds. "It was obvious that he thought no-one could touch him. He divided the patients up into groups, and he'd focus on a different group each day. Again, I didn't even have it as bad as some people. I'd never heard screams like that before. He believed that by torturing people, he could break them, and that then he could re-make them so that they'd be stronger. He thought that was the only way to make us fit to integrate into society."

"Why didn't anyone stop him?" I ask.

"They did, eventually. When word leaked out about what he was doing."

We sit in silence for a moment as I try to take in everything that she's told me.

"He's dead now, isn't he?" I ask finally.

She hesitates, and then she nods.

"So what happened after you were rescued?"

"All his patients were assessed by another doctor," she explains. "A few were sent off for further evaluation. The rest of us were told we'd be moved to another facility and that we had to prepare for release. We were treated well, I think that was mainly because they were worried word would get out about what Doctor Mellor had been doing. Eventually I was given a date and told I'd be coming to live with you. They told us it was over. They said we'd been saved and that we didn't have to worry about Doctor Mellor again."

"But you dream about him?"

She nods.

"Nightmares?"

She nods again.

"This was the first time I've really cried out like that," she says after a moment. "I think, anyway."

"It's the first time I've heard it happen," I tell her.

"It was like I was back there," she replies, and when I look down at her hands I see that they're trembling. "Even when I woke up, I was filled with rage." She turns to me. "What if I'd hurt you?"

"You didn't."

"But I could have!"

"But you didn't," I say firmly, before getting to my feet and limping around the table. After stopping for a moment, I kneel next to her. "You didn't hurt anyone," I point out. "And you won't, either. Everything's going to be fine."

I wait, but she doesn't seem reassured. After a moment, I lean closer, and then I kiss her on the cheek. I wait again, but she's simply staring at me. I don't know why, but finally I lean closer again, and this time I give her a gentle kiss on the lips, just for half a second or so.

Pulling back, I can see the surprise in her eyes.

"I'm not good around people," she says.

"Me neither."

"I remember when I was a kid," she continues, "my parents invited all my aunts and uncles and cousins to the house once, and I hated it. That was the moment when I knew that I wanted to live alone when I got older."

"Me too," I say with a faint smile. "I have that exact same memory. My cousin Ian even -"

"Punched you on the arm?" she suggests.

"Exactly," I reply. "It was that exact moment when I realized how much I hated being around other people. I guess it was the same for both of us, huh?"

I wait, but she seems lost in her thoughts, as if she can't shake the fear.

"Hey," I continue, feeling slightly flustered and embarrassed, "I've got an idea. Something that'll make you feel better."

CHAPTER TWENTY-FOUR

GASPING FOR BREATH, I lean forward and try to steady myself.

"Are you okay?" the other Ann asks, and she sounds breathless too as she puts a hand on my shoulder from behind. "I thought you were going to fall just then."

I turn to her and smile, and then I look out across the vast, glittering lake. It's mid-morning now, about twelve hours after I woke her from that nightmare, and we've finally come out for a mega-run together. My foot feels so much better, and I've decided to take the risk. Ever since all this craziness started, I've been watching the lake from afar, but this is the first time in ages that I've actually made it all the way to the shore. And when I check my watch, I see that I've beaten my personal best time.

"You were right," the other me says, stepping past the noticeboard and heading down to the very edge of the water. "This was a great idea." She uses a hand to shield her eyes from the sun as she looks out across the water. "It's exactly like the lake from my world. I swear, it's as if every tree, every grain of dirt is the same."

I watch her for a moment, and I can't help thinking that she seems very relaxed. For maybe the first time since she arrived, she seems not to have the edge of anger in her soul. When she turns to me, her smile seems natural and unforced.

"I come here to clear my head," I tell her, stepping over to join her. "I guess I don't need to tell you that, huh? But I come here to let all the thoughts leave my mind. It's like -"

"It's like a reset," she says, finishing my sentence for me.

I nod. "Exactly."

"Sorry," she adds, "I shouldn't have done that."

"Done what?"

"Interrupted you like that."

"It's fine. You said exactly what I was going to say."

She smiles, and then there's a brief, comfortable pause between us.

"Do you want to go swimming?" she asks suddenly.

"In the lake?" I hesitate. "I've never -"

"You've never gone in before," she says. "Just like me. Because you're scared?"

"It's a big lake," I point out, "and it's deep. And I've never been the strongest swimmer. I mean, I *can* swim, but I guess you're right. I've always been a bit of a wimp when it comes to things like that." I look out at the water again. "I always worried about what would happen if I got into trouble."

"You're not alone this time," she replies. "Neither am I. This time we've got each other."

***

"I think I'm actually starting to warm up!" I yell as I swim out to join her in the middle of the lake. "It's actually not so bad!"

"It's beautiful," she replies, treading water nearby. She turns and looks around. "I've never seen it from here before. I can't imagine a more beautiful place to live in the whole world."

I turn and follow her gaze, and I have to admit that she's right. From down here in the water, I can't even see the road that runs past the lake. It's as if the whole of human civilization has vanished. I turn and look the other way, and I spot our clothes on the shore, and then I look up and I can just about see the glint of sunlight catching the window of my house. Of *our* house.

"Are you okay there?" she asks.

"I'm fine," I reply, turning back to her just as she reaches out and touches my shoulder to help steady me. "See? I haven't sunk yet!"

"I always wanted to come out here," she says. "I guess I just never managed to pluck up the courage. I always imagined the worst that could possibly happen, like maybe getting my feet snagged in something and ending up sinking."

"I don't feel anything down there at all," I point out, and it's true. Since we left the shore, my feet haven't so much as brushed against a solitary underwater plant.

It's as if we're floating in a vast, bottomless lake.

"It seems crazy to have been so scared for so long," she says. "There's really nothing out here after all. Then again, I guess that's always been one of my biggest problems. In any situation, I always imagine the worst that could happen, and then somehow I assume that it *will*."

"I'm the same," I reply.

She smiles and turns to look away, and for a moment the only sound comes from the water rippling against us as we continue to tread water. I usually find silences pretty awkward, but for the first time I don't actually feel an urge to say anything. I'm just enjoying this moment, as if this is a perfect day.

"Hey," the other me says suddenly, turning back to face me, "I've got an idea. Race you to the shore."

"What?"

"Let's race!" she continues with a grin. "Let's see who's fastest!"

I open my mouth to reply, but suddenly she sets off, crashing through the water. Realizing that I'm already losing ground, I hesitate for a few seconds and then I set off after her. Between us, we're making a lot of noise now, but I guess that's okay. It's not like we're going to disturb anyone out here. It's just us, all alone.

***

"You so would *not* have beaten me," the other me laughs as we make our way along the path that leads to our house. "Sure, I got about five seconds' head start, but I beat you by way more than that. I beat you by seven or eight seconds at least."

"Keep telling yourself that, loser," I reply.

"Watch who you're calling a loser!" Laughing again, she nudges my shoulder.

I immediately nudge her back.

"You're just bitter," she continues. "Don't worry, though, I'll give you another chance. We'll go down again and next time I'll let you be the one with a head start. Bet you anything in the world that I still beat you."

"As if," I tell her, "but you're totally on."

"When we get back inside," she replies, "I'm going to take a shower and then I'm going to cook the most amazing pasta bake you've ever tasted in your life."

"With aubergine?"

"Among other things. I also have a secret ingredient."

"Is it cinnamon? Because if it's cinnamon, then we have the same secret ingredient."

"It's not cinnamon," she replies. "Well, okay, it *is* cinnamon. But I have a magic touch that'll make it better than anything you've ever tasted. You don't mind waiting until after I've showered, though, do you?"

"Of course not. I need to shower too." We walk on for a moment. "We might as well shower together," I add finally. "I mean, it'd save water, right?"

"Are you sure?"

I glance at her. For a moment, I wonder whether I'm doing the right thing, but then I allow myself a faint smile.

"Sure," I say. "And then we should start talking about the living arrangements. That sofa bed can't be good for your back, and I don't want you using it as an excuse when I beat you next time we go to the lake. So maybe you'd like to come and join me in the -"

Suddenly I see an expression of shock in her eyes, and she stops as she sees something ahead of us. Turning, I too am shocked as I see Donna's car parked outside our house. Donna's knocking at the front door, and I immediately feel a flicker of concern as I realize that she's not even due to visit us yet.

"What's she doing here?" the other me asks. "I thought she was going to stay away for a whole month?"

CHAPTER TWENTY-FIVE

"YOU HAVE TO UNDERSTAND," Donna says a short while later, as I sit opposite her at the dining room table, "we're only doing this because we need to correct any mistakes that have been made. As I told the other Ann a few minutes ago, this is really for her own benefit."

"But she's fine!" I say firmly, struggling to contain my sense of panic. "She's been here long enough now for me to see that!"

Donna hesitates, before glancing over her shoulder. Following her gaze, I see that the other me is outside in the yard. She went out there a short while ago, without saying a word, after being given the news by Donna. Now she's sitting on the old fallen log near the treeline, and she has her head in her hands. I want to rush out there and comfort her, but I know that instead I need to find a way to talk Donna out of this decision.

"The investigation in Cottonhurst was only concluded a few days ago," Donna explains, "and the findings in the report..."

She pauses, and when I turn to her I see tears in her eyes.

"Parts of the report are being kept from the public," she continues, "in order to protect the dignity of all the victims. There were rumors about Doctor Mellor for a long time, but the report has uncovered a huge amount of torture and abuse. Some of the investigators themselves have required professional help in order to help them process the horrors that they read about. That's why the government has decided that all former Cottonhurst patients have to be recalled for a proper, thorough psychological examination."

"And how long will that take?" I ask.

"A timeline hasn't been established yet."

"But are we talking days? Weeks?"

I wait, but she doesn't answer.

"Months?" I continue, struggling to hold back tears.

"It'll take as long as it needs to take," Donna explains. "Obviously I can't go into detail, but we've determined that several former Cottonhurst residents have gone on to experience difficulties in their integration."

"What kind of difficulties?"

"Serious difficulties?"

"Violent difficulties?"

"I'm not at liberty to go into detail."

"Have any of them murdered their counterparts in this world?"

"Officially, no link has been determined," she replies. "Unofficially... Yes. There have been several confirmed cases and a dozen that are being looked into right now. We're working with the producers of *Doppelgangers Gone Bad* to access their raw files and see what other mistakes might have been made. These people were already damaged when they came to our world, Ann, but what happened at Cottonhurst pushed them over the edge. Frankly, it's a miracle that the other you has managed to stay so sane. Well, relatively sane, at least."

"She's no danger to anyone," I tell her.

"We're doing this to protect both of you. Every former Cottonhurst resident is being -"

"You don't need to take her away!"

She sighs.

"Send someone to study her here," I continue. "They should see her in her natural environment. They should see her in her home!"

"Not so long ago, you were begging me to take her away."

"That was then!" I snap. "That was before -"

I stop myself just in time. For a moment, I try to think of something I can say or do that will make Donna understand, but I'm already coming up with nothing. From a completely detached point of view, I can completely see why the former Cottonhurst residents need to be re-evaluated. It's just that I don't want the other me to leave. Not now, not when we've been managing to get along so well.

I'll miss her.

"I'm taking her with me today," Donna says finally. "If she passes her new evaluation tests, she'll be back within six months."

"And if she doesn't?" I ask.

"If she doesn't..." She pauses. "If she doesn't," she continues, "then she'll be given the appropriate treatment. At a facility with people who know how to look after her."

"Funny," I reply darkly, "that sounds exactly like what was supposed to be happening at Cottonhurst in the first place."

CHAPTER TWENTY-SIX

"HEY," I SAY AS I stop next to the log and look down at the other me. She still has her head in her hands. "How are you doing out here?"

She looks up at me, and I'm immediately shocked to see that there are tears streaming down her face. Her eyes are red from so much crying, and her hands are trembling.

"It's going to be okay," I say, taking a seat next to her and putting an arm around her shoulder. "You'll be back in no time."

I look out for a moment at the distant lake. A few hours ago we were swimming in that beautiful water, and I began to believe that everything was going to be okay. Now we're about to be torn apart.

"There doesn't seem to be anything we can do to stop this," I continue after a few seconds. "A law has been passed, stating that all former Cottonhurst residents have to go in for further checks. But once those checks are complete, the Rutherford Act remains in place and you'll be sent straight back here. I'll be waiting for you."

Again I wait, but again she says nothing.

"We just have to tough it out," I say finally. "We have to stay strong."

"They won't send me back to you," she replies through gritted teeth.

"What -"

"I won't pass their tests!" she snaps. She looks back toward the house, as if she's worried that Donna might be eavesdropping, and then she turns to me again. "You know I won't. They'll have quotas, there'll be a certain number of people who need to be detained in order for the program to make a profit. And I won't be deemed safe. Don't even try to tell me that I'm wrong."

"I -"

"Did you tell her about last night?" she asks, interrupting me yet again. "Did you tell her about the nightmare, and about the fact that I tried to kill you?"

"I didn't, no."

"Because you knew that it'd be used against me."

"Because it didn't seem relevant."

As soon as I've said those words, I know

how utterly ridiculous they sound. Of course last night is relevant, and in truth I didn't want to say anything that might harm the other Ann's case.

"I'll still have nightmares when I'm taken back," she explains. "I had them at Cottonhurst before, but I was starting to get better after I came here. Now I'm going to another facility, the nightmares will return. I won't be able to stop them."

"So?" I reply. "Nightmares aren't a cast-iron sign of madness. If they were, half the population would be locked away."

"And what if I attack a guard?"

"You won't."

"I can't promise that." She wipes some more tears away. "I could see it in Donna's eyes just now, when she was explaining things to me. She keeps saying that everything will be fine, but I could see in her eyes that she knows I won't ever come back to you. They're going to lock me away forever."

I shake my head.

"When I arrived," she continues, "I'd have been jumping for joy at this news. But now..."

She pauses, before placing a hand on my knee.

"They're going to tear us apart," she adds.

"I won't let them."

"You don't have a choice."

I want to tell her that she's wrong, but deep

down I know that all I can offer is a set of bland, empty promises. The same forces that forced her to come here are now forcing her to leave, and in both cases we're entirely powerless. For a moment I consider suggesting that she could go on the run, that she could hide here and that I'd keep her safe, but I already know that we'd never succeed. She's trapped in the jaws of a giant machine, and there's no way to get her out.

Hearing a bumping sound, I turn and see that Donna has emerged from the house.

"It's time," the other me whispers.

"There has to be another way," I tell her.

I watch her face for a moment, and I see pure hatred in her eyes as she stares at Donna. Then, suddenly, she gets to her feet.

"Wait!" I gasp instinctively.

"No, I'm ready," she replies, her voice suddenly sounding much calmer, as if she's made up her mind. "There's no point delaying things, right? I mean, she'll get the police involved if we refuse to cooperate. No sane person would try fighting this. We have to do what we're told. I have to go to Cottonhurst and let them examine me."

"There has to be a way," I say as I stand and grab her hand, which she instantly pulls away. "You'll be back soon, I promise!"

I try again to take her hand; again, she slips free. She suddenly seems so much colder, as if in some way deep down she's already adjusting to the idea that she has to leave. I was expecting her to kick and scream, to refuse to go. Instead, she seems resigned to what's happening and I suddenly feel as if I'm going to burst into tears.

"Let's get this over with," she says, stepping past me and heading toward Donna's car.

"Wait!" I shout, hurrying after her. "This isn't right! We have to do something!"

***

"I'm glad you're making the right decision," Donna says as she opens the passenger-side door. "There's a process to go through, and at the end of that process you could very well be released and sent back here. You have to hold onto some hope."

She waits for the other me to say something, but there's no response. Instead, the other me simply climbs into the car and pulls the door shut with force.

"I wish I could help more," Donna tells me, "but my hands are tied. This is a universal rule regarding everyone who was at Cottonhurst, it's nothing personal."

"She's not crazy," I reply.

"Let's hope not," she says, "because then she'll be back here eventually. Either way, she's going to get the treatment that she needs. The government is committed to putting things right, Ann. No-one wants to lock anyone up unless it's strictly necessary." She pauses, before heading around to the other side of the car and opening the door. "I'll be in touch when I have some news. You'll have to be patient, though. These things take time."

She climbs into the car, and I look down at Ann and see that she's staring down at her lap. It's almost as if she's deliberately avoiding looking at me. I want to go and hug her, to tell her that I'll be waiting for her to come back, but at the same time I feel as if she'd just push me away. And as the car pulls away and heads along the road, I feel as if a part of me is being stolen.

Finally she's gone, and I'm left standing all alone in the yard with tears in my eyes.

CHAPTER TWENTY-SEVEN

MORE RAIN.

I swear, I don't remember there ever being a time when more rain fell in such a short period of time. There's been rain almost every day for a month, and now a light drizzle is tapping at the window. I glance over from my laptop, but night has fallen and all I see is darkness. I can still *hear* the rain, however, and somehow the sound make me feel more aware than ever of the fact that I'm so far from civilization.

And the house feels so empty.

I turn and look around, but there's no sign of life. Even Sheba has stayed out tonight, which is unusual when there's bad weather. I guess maybe she's picked up on all the craziness of late, and she's decided to steer clear of the house until everything has settled down. Frankly, I can't say that I blame her, although I hope she comes back eventually. I never used to feel lonely here, not before the other me came. Now I can barely stand to be here.

Hearing a bumping sound, I turn and look over my shoulder. For a fraction of a second, I expect to see the other Ann coming through from the kitchen, and my heart skips a beat before I remember that she's not here. I still watch the empty doorway for a few seconds, before turning back to my laptop.

I need to get on with some work, but my mind is already starting to wander.

Opening a browser window, I bring up a news page and try to find some mention of the Cottonhurst incident. Eventually I find a very vague mention of some doppelgangers being recalled due to some 'irregularities', but it's quite clear that the news outlets are giving out only the bare minimum of information. They still aren't mentioning Doctor Mellor, and I feel a flicker of anger at the thought of all these horrors getting covered up. Meanwhile, hundreds – maybe even thousands – of people are being rounded up and sent back for re-evaluation.

She'll be back soon.

I'm assuming the worst, as usual.

She'll pass the tests with flying colors, and soon she'll be right back here.

Suddenly I hear a creaking sound. I turn and

look toward the window, and a moment later the sound returns. I wait, but now all I hear is the sound of rain coming down, although after a moment I get to my feet and head across the room. When I reach the window, I can only see my own reflection, so I switch the lights off and plunge the room into darkness, and after a moment my eyes adjust and I'm able to see the darkness of the yard outside.

There's no sign of movement, but those two creaks seemed very insistent, and I can't shake a tingling sense of concern.

I pause, and then I head over to the door and slide it open. Stepping out onto the porch, I immediately feel a light rain falling against my face, so I stop and look out at the yard. I keep telling myself that there's no-one else here, that I'm just imagining things, but for a moment I simply stand and watch and listen. As the rain continues to fall, however, I start to realize that the sounds must have just been some part of the house creaking in the wind. Maybe the water system, set up by the other me, isn't quite as sturdy as it appeared. I'll have to go and take a look at that in the morning.

Once I'm satisfied that I'm all alone out here, I step back and slide the door shut.

I feel as if I'm in danger of losing my mind. Maybe I'm the one who should have been carted off to Cottonhurst for evaluation, and the other me should have stayed here. Then again, as I head back to my desk I tell myself that I really need to stay calm and just wait to hear back from Donna. There's still a real chance that everything will be okay.

Realizing that I'm in no mood to work, I close my laptop and switch the TV on. The signal came back a while earlier. In fact, everything seems to have gone back to normal now.

Almost on autopilot, I flick through to one of the higher channels, and then as I take a seat I bring up the latest episode of *Doppelgangers Gone Bad*.

I shouldn't be watching this garbage, and I feel faintly nauseous as the title sequence begins. At the same time, I want to remind myself of all this paranoid nonsense. I can't believe that I actually used to watch this stuff and believe it was true. I filled my head with the worst possible ideas, and I let those ideas run rampant in my imagination. I sat here night after night, letting myself believe the absolute worst, until I very nearly pushed the other me away. The problem is, shows like *Doppelgangers Gone Bad* are so expertly put together, it's almost impossible to keep from getting sucked in.

Suddenly I hear another, louder bump nearby, this time seemingly coming from inside the house.

Startled, I get to my feet. Grabbing the remote, I put the TV onto mute and then I listen. All

I hear now is silence, but I swear I heard something actually in the house, as if someone shoved a door open. The hairs are standing up on the back of my neck, and I can feel a cold sweat starting to creep across my body.

I have to stay calm.

I can't let myself go crazy.

I need to keep my head together.

After a moment, I realize that I've been holding my breath. I force myself to breathe deep, then I hesitate for a few more seconds before turning back to un-mute the TV.

Suddenly I spot something moving out of the corner of my eye, and I turn just in time to see a human figure running through the darkness and slamming against the patio door. For a fraction of a second I have no idea what's happening, but then to my astonishment I see that Donna's out there. She looks utterly horrified as she starts banging against the window, and I can't hear what she's saying but she's shouting something at me as rain continues to pour down.

CHAPTER TWENTY-EIGHT

"SHE COULD HAVE KILLED us," Donna gasps as she continues to dab at her face with a towel. She's soaking wet, and there's mud all over her coat. "She just grabbed the wheel and..."

Her voice trails off, and for a moment she stares into space as if she's reliving the moment yet again. She's clearly in shock, and I can't say that I blame her.

"She just grabbed the wheel," she continues finally, "and forced us straight off the road at full speed. We so nearly hit a tree, and then we went thudding down into a ditch. I was wearing my seat belt, but my head hit something and the next thing I know, I woke up and I was all alone in the car."

"And are you sure you don't know where the other Ann went?" I ask.

"She was just gone!" she replies. "I thought maybe she'd come back here."

"I haven't seen her," I explain, before looking back over toward the window. "If the crash was several hours ago, she's had more than enough time to get back here. If that was her plan, at least."

"My phone's no use," she says. "It's had no signal since the crash, I think it must have been damaged. I need to use yours."

"I still don't have one," I tell her. "I told you, it was stolen when I got attacked."

"Then I need to use your internet!"

I head over to my desk and open my laptop. Once I've typed in the password, I bring up a browser window, only to find that the internet has stopped again. It's just like before, when it mysteriously failed to work for a while. I try a few things, hoping to get it back up and running, and then I turn to Donna.

"It's no good," I stammer. "I can't get it working."

"Let me try!" she snaps breathlessly, pushing me aside before starting to tap furiously at the keyboard. She's muttering a few curses as she struggles, and I can't help noticing that she's still dripping muddy water everywhere.

I guess maybe now wouldn't be a good time to ask her to stop.

"So you're telling me that we're stuck out

here?" she says finally, turning to me. "Seriously? Is there no way for us to contact the civilized world?"

I try to think of something, but she's basically correct. And then, in a moment of clarity, I remember that there might just be one chance.

"I have a bike," I tell her. "It's in the basement, I haven't used it for years, but -"

"Go and get it!"

"It's probably rusty and -"

"Go and get it!" she shouts, interrupting me again.

"It's pouring with rain out there," I point out.

"Go and get your goddamn bike," she says firmly. "I have to report what's happened. I have to call the police!"

"Isn't that a little drastic?" I suggest.

"She tried to kill me!"

"I'm sure that wasn't her intention," I tell her. "She probably just panicked, that's all. I don't think she'd ever actually have tried to hurt you."

"She can explain that to the police," Donna says firmly. "She's a screwed-up bitch and she belongs behind bars in a hospital! Now are you going to go and fetch that bike, or do I have to tear this house apart and find it myself?"

I open my mouth to tell her that everything will be alright, but then I realize that maybe this isn't the proper moment. She looks red in the face, as if she's ready to explode with rage, so I figure that I need to at least stall for time while I try to work out what's happening.

"I'll be right back," I say finally, before turning and heading over to the back door.

Grabbing my coat, I step out into the rain. As I make my way down the steps, I can't help glancing around, watching the darkness in case there's any sign of the other me. I don't see anyone, but I can't shake the feeling that I'm being watched as I slip my arms into the coat and head around to the door that leads down into the basement. Even as I fish the keys from my pocket and open the padlock, I feel as if at any moment I might suddenly feel a familiar hand touching my shoulder from behind.

Once I'm in the basement, I switch the light on and then I head down the steps. The first thing I notice is that everything down here has been completely re-organized. I guess the other me really got serious when it came to tidying up and getting down to work. When I last saw the bike – admittedly, at least a year ago – it was resting against the wall near the electricity meter, but now there are several boxes in that spot. I start looking around, and finally I see the bike over at the far end of the basement.

I make my way over, although I stop suddenly as I hear a brief, loud bump coming from above. Looking up at the ceiling, I wait in case there's another sound, but now all I hear is the rain still coming down outside.

I head to the bike and pull it away from the wall, and then I take a moment to wipe away the worst of the muck and cobwebs. The chain looks to be in decent condition, and the tires are fine, so I guess I can't use anything like that as an excuse to not cycle through the rainy night and get help. I guess I could sabotage the tires, but that would feel wrong, so I start wheeling the bike back across the basement as I try to think of some other way that I can delay helping Donna call the police.

And then I stop as I see that one corner of the basement has been completely cleared, with an old sheet having been hung from the window as a kind of curtain.

I hesitate, telling myself that there's no reason to be concerned, but then I wheel the bike over and reach out to pull the curtain aside. Somehow, I can't shake the feeling that the curtain has been put up in an attempt to hide something. As soon as I step around the curtain, I see that my suspicions were correct, and I let out a shocked gasp as I see what the other me has created down here.

There are photos of me pinned to the wall.

Scores and scores of photos.

And drawings too.

I don't want to use the word 'shrine', but that's certainly what this place looks like. I step forward, too shocked to really know how to react, and I can only stare at all the pictures. After a moment, I notice that some of the photos show me asleep in my bedroom, and I realize that the other me must have loaded them onto the computer and then printed them out. She's been taking photos of me while I'm asleep, and when I look up toward the top of the wall I'm astonished to see several photos of me that were taken while I was in the shower.

She must have been peering through the window. There are marks on some of the photos, and I peer closer. Sure enough, the other me has drawn ragged lines on a few of the shots that show my naked body, and I realize to my horror that it's as if she's been drawing scars onto my side, trying to make me look like her.

There are notes, too, and I see that she's written little comments about some of the pictures.

"You're so beautiful without the war," I read out loud from one. "You're perfect."

I feel a shiver pass along my spine, and after a moment I take a step back.

Suddenly I hear another bump from upstairs, and then another. Then I stand and listen to the sound of the rain, and after a moment I turn and look back at the wall of photos and text.

She's insane.

No, not insane.

She just needs help.

Turning, I start wheeling the bike toward the steps. This time, I'm no longer trying to work out how to delay my journey. Instead, I'm rapidly coming to realize that perhaps the other me *does* need some help after all. I've had my suspicions, on and off, but now it's really clear that there's something wrong with her.

I struggle to get the bike up the steps, and then I hurry around to the back door. I rest the bike against the wall and take a moment to check that the light on the front works, and then I head back into the house.

"Hey!" I call out. "I got it! If I set off now, I can reach town before the sun comes up!"

Stopping in the middle of the front room, I look around, but there's no sign of Donna. I'd expected to find her still angrily trying to get my laptop to work, but I don't see or hear any sign of her.

"Donna?" I say cautiously. "Where are you?"

I wait for a response, and then I start making my way across the room. Reaching the desk, I see that my laptop has been sent crashing to the floor, where it's resting on its side.

I glance over my shoulder, and then I step through to the doorway and look into the kitchen.

Gasping, I see Donna's dead face staring back at me from the far corner. She's been impaled on the rod that the other me had attached to the crude, bodged-together water filtration system. The rod's spiked tip is poking out about a meter from the center of Donna's chest, with blood glistening on the black metal.

"No," I whisper, as I step forward, but then I stop again as I realize that I'm far too late.

I begin to turn away, but suddenly the lights flick off and I'm left standing in darkness. I hurry to the wall and try the switch, but the lights don't work and when I look over at the oven I see that the clock has turned off, which can only mean one thing.

The other me has cut the power to the house.

CHAPTER TWENTY-NINE

STANDING COMPLETELY STILL IN the dark kitchen, I listen to the sound of falling rain and I wait for some hint that the other me is coming closer.

There are only two ways she could have cut the power like this. The first would be to disconnect the meter down in the basement, and the second would be to throw the switch that's in a closet in my bedroom. I have no idea which approach she's taken, but either means that she must be in the house and she must be close.

I take a couple of steps back, and then I reach out and carefully slide the largest knife from the block on the counter.

I try to tell myself that I'm overreacting, that the other me isn't actually dangerous. Then I look over at Donna's dead body, and I realize that I'm dealing with a murderer. I strengthen my hold on the knife, and then I turn and look at the open doorway that leads out into the front room.

She's waiting for me.

I have two options. I can either wait here until she comes, or I can go out there and face her. For a moment, too scared to move, I consider trying to hide, but then I take a deep breath and tell myself that I have to go out there and make her realize that she's losing her mind. She's never seemed completely unreasonable, and I figure there's still a chance that I can talk her around.

I slip the knife behind my belt, so that it's not too obvious, and then I start cautiously making my way toward the door.

When I look through at the front room, I don't see any sign of her. The room is dark, of course, so she could be lurking in the shadows, but so far she doesn't seem to be here at all. Still, I know she can't have gone far. It's not as if she would have cut the power and then just wandered off into the forest.

I swallow hard.

"Hey," I say finally, and I can immediately hear my voice trembling with fear. "It's me. Can you come out so I can talk to you?"

I wait, but all I hear is the rain.

"Everything's going to be okay," I continue.

"We're on the same side here, we just need to figure out what to do next. I know you must be scared, but..."

My voice trails off.

"But we can do this if we stick together," I add. "Just come out and sit down and we can come up with a plan. No matter how scared you are, you must realize that this isn't the right choice."

I look around the room, watching the shadows for any sign of movement. Maybe I'm going crazy, but I swear I can feel her watching me.

Reaching out, I try the light switch again, but of course it still doesn't work.

Suddenly I hear a clicking sound nearby, and I spin around and watch the shadows. At the same time, I reach down for the knife that's tucked into my belt, but I don't pull it out. Not yet. I don't want to scare the other me too much.

I wait, but there's no sign of her, and I'm already starting to doubt that the clicking sound was even real.

My heart is pounding so hard, I feel as if it's about to burst out of my chest at any moment.

"Please," I say out loud, "just talk to me. What other options do you have? The sooner we talk, the sooner we can come up with a plan. And I think a plan is exactly what we need at the moment, don't you?"

I wait.

The rain is still falling outside.

Sighing, I realize that maybe this approach isn't going to work. I'm certain she must be close, but I'm starting to wonder whether maybe she's down in the basement and I'm simply talking into thin air. I look around one more time, and then I start making my way across the room, heading toward the back door. When I get there, I'm relieved and somewhat surprise to see the bike still leaning against the wall, so I glance over my shoulder one more time before opening the door and stepping out into the rain.

Immediately, I see that the bike's tires have been slashed.

Looking around, I still don't see any sign of the other me, but it's obvious that she's been out here. I didn't hear the door at all, which means that either she was supernaturally quiet, or she hasn't been inside the house since she killed Donna. If she planned to actually hurt me, she'd have been able to make her move by now, so I can't shake the feeling that instead she's simply panicking. But if she won't talk to me, I'm going to *have* to get help.

I take one final look back into the house, and then I turn and hurry down the steps.

Making my way out across the rainy yard, I'm already soaked by the time I get halfway. I start picking up the pace as I reach the start of the road, and I know that it's going to take me hours and hours to get to town. Then again, if I strike lucky and manage to hitch a lift, I could be safe within an hour or two.

"Stop!" a voice suddenly yells.

Startled, I spin around and see the other me standing on the porch, her silhouette just about visible in the darkness.

For a moment, I consider turning and running, but then I realize that I might be getting another chance to talk to her. If I can talk her round, I can still help her.

I take a few steps back across the yard, and then I stop as I wait for her to make her move. Reaching down, I double-check that the knife is still tucked in my belt, but I don't take it out, not yet.

I want the other me to think that I trust her.

I wait, but she says nothing. She's the one who called after me, but now she doesn't seem to have anything to say.

"What did you do?" I call out finally, before taking a few more steps forward. I stare up at the silhouette on the porch, but she still doesn't reply. "If you're scared," I continue, "I can help you, but this isn't the way."

Again, I wait, and again she says nothing.

Just as I'm about to speak to her again, she turns and heads back into the house. Once she's out of view, I realize that I still have the option to run. A moment later, however, the lights come back on, so

I guess that in some strange way the other me is maybe inviting me to go inside with her. I check the knife again, and then I head up the steps and into the front room.

Immediately, I realize I can hear the sound of her sobbing in the kitchen.

I make my way to the doorway and look through, and I see the other me standing with her forehead pressed against the wall. She's weeping uncontrollably, and for a moment I genuinely don't know what to say to her. Finally, unable to come up with a better option, I step closer and put a hand on her shoulder.

"I couldn't do it!" she blurts out suddenly, turning to me with tear-filled eyes. "As soon as we started driving away, I -"

"I know," I say, trying to sound calm and reassuring.

"It never would have worked!" she whimpers. "I was dumb to think I could just go there and then eventually I'd come out again and everything would be okay and -"

"I know," I say, "but -"

Before I can finish, she turns and slams her head against the wall. She tries again, but this time I'm quick and I manage to pull her away. She tries to slip free, but I put my arms around her to hold her in place, and finally she stops struggling and instead rests her face against my shoulder.

"It didn't have to be like this," she continues, "but there's still time. We can come up with something."

"I don't know what," I reply, and my mind is racing as I try to think of some way for us to fix this situation. "We need to think."

"I'm so stupid!"

"Just stay calm and we'll work it out."

"Calm?"

She steps back and stares at me with an expression of pure horror, and then she turns and looks over at Donna's dead body.

"Calm?" she says again. "How can you even use that word?"

"It won't help us to panic," I point out. "We need clear heads."

She stares at Donna's corpse for a moment, as if she's lost in her own thoughts, and then she turns to me. I want to tell her that we'll be fine, but at the same time I can't ignore the fact that she's murdered someone.

"I panicked," she says finally, and she's starting to sob again. "In that car, and then when I got back here, I just panicked and I didn't know what to do."

"I know," I reply, before stepping closer and putting my arms around her, and holding her tight. "I understand."

She weeps against my shoulder again. I try

to work out what I should do next, but after a moment I notice our reflection in the window, and I see that the other me is holding something behind her back. To my horror, I realize that she's got one of the knives. Sure enough, when I look over toward the counter, I see that there are now two knives missing from the block. And as I watch, she's slowly sliding the knife out from behind her belt.

"Please, no," I whisper.

Suddenly I push her away and reach down, grabbing my own knife and holding it up. She instantly does the same, and for a moment we stare at each other before – finally – she lunges at me and screams.

CHAPTER THIRTY

SLAMMING INTO THE EDGE of the doorway, I let out a cry as I try to force the other me away. She's holding my arm tight, and after a moment the blade of her knife flashes past my face. In an instant, I turn and throw her through the doorway, sending her clattering into one of the chairs with such force that she topples over and hits the floor.

Suddenly feeling the knife slip from my hand, I reach down to pick it back up, only for the other me to swing her left foot out and kick the knife across the room.

I hurry past her, but she grabs my leg and pulls me down.

Screaming, I turn and use my other leg to kick her hard in the face. She lets out a cry of pain and falls back, giving me enough time to turn again and scramble toward the knife. I reach out to grab the handle, but at the last moment the other me slams into me from behind and gasps as she pulls me back.

Turning, I see that she still has a knife in her right hand. I grab her arm and smash it against the side of the sofa, but she keeps the knife tightly gripped so I have to try two more times before she finally lets go. She turns to me, and I quickly slam my elbow into her face before trying once again to grab my knife. This time I succeed, and I turn to face her.

She screams as she throws a vase at my face. I try to duck out of the way, but the vase hits me on the side of the head and I cry out as I drop down to my knees. For a moment, I feel as if I'm about to pass out, but I manage to stumble to my feet and raise the knife. As I do so, the other me grabs me by the arm and swings me around, trying to throw me against the wall. I manage to steady myself at the last moment, and instead I turn and try to push her back down to the floor.

We grapple for a moment, until suddenly she throws all her weight against me and we crash against the patio door.

The glass instantly shatters and we fall through together, landing in a shower of tiny shards that come raining down all around us. I land on my back, and the other me lands straight on top of me, but I quickly throw her aside. At the same time, I feel hundreds of glass shards cutting into my legs and back, but I don't even have time to register the pain properly. Instead, I turn and see that the other me has landed close to a knife, so I lunge past her and try to grab it before she gets a chance.

"No!" she yells, and suddenly she slams her head against mine, knocking me back against the frame of the shattered window.

Before I have a chance to get to my feet, she grabs me from behind and swings me around, and then she pushes me off the porch and sends me slamming down against the steps. I roll to the muddy ground, and when I try to get up I feel a sharp pain slicing through my left side, as if I've broken a couple of ribs. At least I managed to get the knife. Rain is pouring down all around me, and for a few seconds I simply don't have the energy to lift myself up.

Suddenly I hear her hurrying down the steps behind me.

I start to turn, but she throws herself against my back. I fall flat on my face, straight in the mud, and then I roll onto my back just as she lands on top of me, straddling me and raising the knife high in the air. I stare, waiting for her to bring the blade crashing down against my chest, but for a moment she hesitates. I can see the fear and shock in her eyes, as if she's having second thoughts, and in a flash I realize that this might be my last chance to save myself.

With the last of my strength, I grab her by the waist and throw her to one side. She gasps and slams down on her back, letting go of her knife in the process. I grab the knife and turn to push her against the ground, but at that exact moment she tries to get up and rush at me. And as she does she, she crashes against the knife, and I watch with horror as the blade slices straight into her chest.

She freezes, her eyes wide open as she stares at me.

I look down at the knife.

I'm still holding the handle. Rain is pouring down, but there's not actually any blood around the spot on the other Ann's shirt where the blade ran into her. For a moment, I start to wonder whether somehow there's been some kind of miracle that's keeping her alive.

Suddenly she gasps, and when I look at her face I see that blood is dribbling from one corner of her mouth.

"No!" I shout, just as she slumps back down.

The knife slides out of her chest, and I watch as rain hits the blade and starts washing the blood away. More blood, however, is already spreading across the front of her shirt.

"I didn't mean that!" I gasp, as I see the fear in her eyes. "It was an accident, I swear!"

Her lips move slightly, as if she's trying to say something, but she can't get the words out.

"I'm going to get help!" I tell her, before starting to get up. "I'll find someone who can -"

Before I can finish, she grabs my arm, holding me in place. I look back down at her, and as I do so I feel her give my arm a very gentle squeeze.

"This wasn't supposed to happen," I continue, as I see that she's struggling to keep her eyes open. "This isn't how it was supposed to end! You have to believe me! I never wanted to hurt you, I was just trying to protect myself! Please, tell me you know that!"

I wait, but she says nothing. After a moment, however, she squeezes my arm again.

"I didn't want to hurt you!" I sob. "I was just defending myself, that's all. That's the only reason I had the knife! I know you understand! Please, just tell me!"

Her mouth opens slightly, and then her body shudders a little.

I wait.

She's not moving.

I watch as more rain hits her face. She doesn't even blink as drops fall against her eyes, and I'm suddenly filled with shock at the thought that she might be dead.

"No!" I yell, grabbing her shoulders and shaking her, trying to bring her back. "You can't die! I need you here! I won't let you die, you have to come back to me! You can't leave me alone!"

I try resuscitating her, and then I try shaking her again, but nothing works. Deep down, I know that she's gone, but sheer panic is filling my mind and all I can do is keep shaking her in the desperate hope that somehow I can get her back. I can't imagine living here without her, not now. Not after everything we've been through together.

"Come back!" I scream. "You have to come back to me! I can't live without you!"

CHAPTER THIRTY-ONE

DROPPING TO MY KNEES in the front room, I stare at the other me's corpse.

I've dragged her into the house and set her in one of the armchairs. I know full well that what I'm doing is weird, but it's not as if I could have just left her out there in the rain. And now, as I sit in silence and look at her face, I'm starting to feel strangely calm.

Her eyes are open.

There's blood smeared at one corner of her mouth.

She's soaking wet, with hair matted and stuck to one side of her face.

There's more blood on her shirt.

She's really, truly dead.

After a moment, I crawl closer and lean

toward her, and I slowly place a hand on the side of her face. Her skin is so cold and clammy, but she doesn't 'feel' dead yet. I don't even know what I mean by that; I guess it's just that she still feels 'real'. I run my hand up the side of her face, and then I start to slowly pull her hair aside and make it neater. I think she'd want to look neat, even now. I think she'd be grateful to me for doing this.

"I was starting to think that we'd be a team," I tell her, surprising myself a little. I hadn't expected to start talking to her corpse. "Is that strange? It seemed easier, somehow, that we were going to have each other. Two heads are better than one, right?"

I smile at that little joke.

Would she have smiled too, if I'd thought of the joke while she was still alive?

I can't believe that neither of us ever came up with that.

"I really *was* only defending myself," I continue. "I think you understood that, right at the end. It was just bad luck that you happened to sit up while I was holding the knife. I really think that, if you'd survived, we'd have been able to talk things through. We'd have been okay, once we'd dealt all the misunderstandings. I know we would. We'd have been fine out here together, living in this house and just getting on with things." I smile, as tears once again fill my eyes. "We'd have been happy."

I wait, holding my breath.

Deep down, I'm still hoping for a miracle, for the other me to suddenly twitch slightly and turn to me. But there aren't going to be any miracles. Not now, and not ever. She's really gone. I'm going to miss her so much.

Even though I know that this is weird, I lean close and give her a hug.

AMY CROSS

CHAPTER THIRTY-TWO

One month later...

"THANK YOU FOR COMING in today, Ms. Garland," Detective Warner says as he leads me along the corridor. "There are just a couple of things I needed to talk to you about."

"It's fine," I reply, although – as I pass an open door and glance into the busy office – I wince at the sheer noise of this place. There are so many people talking, some of them even yelling at one another.

I just want to get this done, and get home.

"Ms. Garland?"

Startled, I turn and see that Warner's watching me from a door up ahead. I look around for a moment, and then I realize that I must have zoned out for a moment.

"Sorry," I mutter, as I head through the door, into an interview room.

I immediately freeze. When Warner called the other day, he said he simply needed to update me on the investigation, but this is slowly starting to feel like something more official. I turn, just as he shuts the door, sealing us into the room. At least I can no longer hear the noise from the office, although I still feel as if I want to run.

It's okay, I tell myself.

Everyone believed what I told them.

I told them the truth.

"How are you holding up?" he asks.

"Fine. Thank you."

"It's not weird, still living in that house after all that's happened?"

I shake my head.

"It must be strange coming into town like this, though," he continues. "I hear you tend to stay away from civilization."

"I'm very busy," I reply, craning my neck to try to see the files he's examining at the desk. "I work a lot."

"Join the club." He sifts through a few sheets of paper, none of which I can really make out, and then he turns to me. "Your cuts seem a lot better."

I nod.

He hesitates, and then he turns to me.

"I wanted you to know," he says finally, "that we're going to be closing the case on what happened to you. Now, that's not my decision, but we're stretched beyond breaking point and certain cases are being given priority over others. As of today, the file on the incident at your house is going to be archived." He stares at me for a moment. "I should probably inform you at this point that I argued quite strongly that the case should remain open for a little while longer."

I wait for him to continue, but he seems to be watching me quite intently, as if he's studying my reaction. To be honest, I'm simply trying to hide my sense of relief.

"That's... good," I say finally. "I guess."

"Yes, I suppose it is," he replies. "For you."

I wait again, and I'm starting to feel a little uncomfortable. I can't shake the feeling that Warner wants to say something else, but that he's holding back. I glance at the door, and I want to ask if I can leave now, but I don't want to seem too eager.

"I went through your statement," he says finally, "about what happened that night. On the night that the other you died. I must admit, I regret the fact that I won't have the chance to go into the matter in a more thorough manner."

I force a smile, hoping that this is the normal response.

"We finally received the autopsy report for Donna Martin," he continues, taking one of the files and taking another look at its contents. "Everything's been so backed up lately. But they got the results, and we now have a cause of death."

"I didn't think there was much doubt about that," I reply.

"Neither did I." He flips to the second page of the file. "Donna Martin had a history of heart trouble. Now, the coroner can't be certain, but he states in his report that the cause of death was *not* actually the large spike that was driven through her chest. He believes that, following her strenuous journey back to your house from her crashed car, she actually suffered a fatal heart attack."

I raise a skeptical eyebrow.

"A heart attack?"

"Indeed." He turns back to the first page of the report, and then closes it altogether. "The coroner's theory, as unlikely as it might sound, is that she suffered the cardiac arrest and died almost instantly. It would appear that she then fell back and, in an extremely unfortunate series of events, landed on the spike."

I stare at him, convinced that this has to be a joke.

"I know," he says finally. "Crazy, right?"

"That's..."

For a moment, in my mind's eye, I try to

imagine that happening. I see Donna clutching her chest and stumbling back, maybe struggling to stay upright. And then, as she dies, she falls backward and the spike goes straight through her chest.

I blink.

"So maybe she wasn't murdered after all," Warner continues, "which puts a different complexion on the evening, does it not?"

"I think it sounds... unlikely," I suggest.

"I know. I've read your statement about everything that happened after the other you showed up. About your suspicions."

"I'm not saying I'm totally right about all of that," I tell him, struggling to find the right words, "but I find it hard to believe that Donna just dropped dead and landed on the spike."

"It's a tough one to get your head around," he replies, before grabbing a clear plastic bag and opening it. "By the way, you might be interested in this."

I open my mouth to ask what he means, but to my surprise I see that he's taking out my old phone.

"We recovered it in a raid about thirty miles away. We were investigating some robberies." He holds the phone out toward me. "Here, take it," he adds. "It's yours."

I take the phone, and I can't deny that it's the one I lost after I was attacked in the forest.

"A man named Andrew Lucas has been arrested," Warner explains. "He's already confessed to multiple attacks in the area. He seems to be some kind of itinerant thief, he steals what he can from his victims and in some cases he leaves them to die. He's a drug addict, basically. It looks as if he's the one who attacked you that day. Not the other you."

I swallow hard as I examine the phone. I try to switch it on, but of course the battery's dead.

"And I checked with your ISP," Warner continues. "They've confirmed a major fault on your line. Your internet connection would have been sporadically out for quite some time. Your TV might have been included in that too."

Turning to him, I feel a flicker of fear in my chest.

"All of which," he adds, "makes me wonder what really happened at your house, Ms. Garland. What the other you *really* did. Because it would seem that most, if not all, of your suspicions were unfounded."

"The shrine in the basement," I reply, "and the slashed bike tires, and -"

"I'm not saying she wasn't *weird*," he says, holding his hands up, "not at all. I'm just saying that she might not have been quite the murderer that you've painted her out to be. I'm saying that you might have let yourself get a little carried away with your fears."

"No," I reply, "that's..."

My voice trails off.

"That's impossible," I continue finally. "I mean, she was..."

Again, I'm not quite sure what to say.

"She was..."

I swallow hard.

"I think'd like to leave now," I say finally, as Warner continues to stare at me. "If that's alright with you."

"You're absolutely free to go," he replies, getting up and heading over to the door, which he then pulls open. "For now."

I want to say something, to tell him that he's wrong, but I'm not sure he'd believe anything I told him. As I stand up and make my way to the door, I feel as if I should say something to defend myself, but I can't quite find the words.

"And it was *really* self-defense?" he whispers, leaning a little closer to me. "You can tell me now. Off the record. The one part of all of this that I don't understand is how you two ended up fighting. I can just about get my head around the rest. She went off with Donna, but then maybe she panicked and came back, maybe she felt she couldn't go back to Cottonhurst. Fine, I get that. It was pretty rough of them to insist on her going back to the same place where she was originally held but, hey, bureaucracy can be a bitch. But how did you end up fighting?"

I open my mouth to reply, but for a moment no words emerge from my mouth.

Instead, I think back to that awful night. I found Donna's body, and I assumed that the other me had killed her. Now, finally, I realize that *she* must have assumed the same thing about *me*. She must have returned to the house and seen Donna's corpse, and assumed that I'd lost my mind.

And then there was the knife I saw behind her back. Maybe *she* saw that *I* had a knife too. Maybe we each thought that the other had gone nuts. Maybe she thought she was defending herself, and I thought I was defending myself, and we ended up fighting and crashing through that window and then...

For a moment, I think back to the moment she died, to the fear and shock in her eyes.

"Are you sure you don't want to sit down and talk to me about this?" Warner asks. "Think how good it'd feel to get the truth out. No more stress. No more panic. Just the honest, unvarnished truth. It could even be off the record, at least for now. Think of me as a friend. Think of me as someone you can trust."

I turn to him. For a moment, I imagine taking him up on his offer, but I quickly realize that he's just trying to trick me.

"I'm sorry," I say finally, "but it's really

getting late and I have a long bike ride ahead. I think I'd like to leave now."

EPILOGUE

One year later...

THIS IS PERFECT.

Sheba purrs on the desk as I sit tapping at the laptop. I've got a big commission lined up for a client, and I need to get the last pieces worked out before I submit the finished design of Friday. I'm not in any danger of missing the deadline, of course. I simply need to work solidly and steadily over the next few days, and then I should be finished well in advance. I've got everything I need.

Except, I keep stopping for short periods.

Turning, I look around the front room. I've always loved solitude, ever since I was a kid. Lately, however, I've started to wish that the silence could be broken occasionally. I mean, sure, Sheba makes some noise, and there's also the rustle of trees outside the house, but otherwise the house remains pretty quiet. Day after day, I rattle around in here and I don't see another living soul. And while that's fine most of the time, there are these little blips – little moments like this – when I actually miss having someone else around.

Dumb of me, I know.

But it's true.

After a moment, I realize I can hear a distant buzzing sound.

I turn and look out the window. At first, I see only the gravel driveway that leads off between the trees. Still, the buzzing sound is getting louder, and I know exactly what that means. Getting to my feet, I step away from the desk and head toward the front door. As I go, the television on the far wall flickers to life. I have it set to switch on at precisely 7.30am, with the aim being to force myself to watch the news for a few minutes. This might make me sound weird, but I like seeing what the rest of the world is up to. I like keeping track of the idiots.

The front door slides open and I step out onto the porch, just as the postal drone flies into view. I can't help smiling as I see the drone bringing its little load containing my weekly mail. In the absence of any other human contact, I've come to rather like seeing the drone. I'm probably totally sad, but I almost feel as if the drone's becoming my friend.

"Hey," I say, as the drone drops my mail directly into my hands. "Have a fun journey home, little guy."

Ignoring me, the drone turns and starts buzzing off back toward the gravel path. It's a cute little machine, and I quite like the thought of it zooming away through the forest, heading back to the delivery office several miles away. As I turn and head back into the house, I feel a flicker of regret that it'll be another week before I see the drone again. Still, it's nice to have something to look forward to.

As I step through the door, I hear a faint meowing and I glance down just in time to see Sheba jumping off the sofa and coming over to me. I think she's starting to get a little old now. She's going gray around her mouth and ears, and she spends a lot more time inside than ever before. In fact, she spends most of her time snoozing on the sofa, and as she slinks closer I can't help noticing that she seems to be walking a little stiffly. I guess maybe her hips are a little painful.

"Want some food?" I say as I set the mail down unopened. I grab a box from the counter and head over to the bowl in the corner.

Of course, half of yesterday's food is scattered nearby. Sheba's a messy eater, and she won't touch anything that's fallen out of the bowl.

"You're such a messy cat," I point out with a smile, as I fill her bowl again. "You're lucky you've got me to clean up after you."

Heading back over to the counter, I note that it's getting quite empty. Fortunately my next food delivery is coming tomorrow, again in an automated vehicle. My order rarely changes. Sheba and I both have our habits, and we stick to them each and every month. Once you've found something you like, why change? Well, I usually sneak one or two little unusual items into each order, just to experiment a little.

I grab the letters again, figuring that I should just open them now rather than letting them fester. As I head back to my desk, I glance at the television, which is running on mute. I shudder at the sight of thousands of people crowded into a busy street, and then I stop at the desk and remove the letter from inside one of the newly-arrived envelopes.

And then I freeze.

Glancing back at the silent television, I realize that the 'crowd' on the screen seems agitated. The camera shots are jerky and chaotic, as if something's happening. Feeling a flicker of dread in my chest, I realize that my fellow humans must have done something idiotic again. I watch the screen for a moment longer, but the red banner at the bottom of the image merely mentions the location. My first thought is that this must be the result of some terrorist attack, and then it occurs to me that perhaps some political figure is trying to stir up a crowd. Then, I wonder whether perhaps this is just some kind of music festival, or a demonstration against something, or one of those revolting 'flash mob' things that I read about a few years ago.

But then the image changes again, and I see that there's a vast, bright light burning straight through the center of the street, just a few feet above the ground.

I tell myself that this peculiar sight is the result of some kind of lens flare, but then the camera view changes slightly and I see that there's actually a ribbon-like strip of lightning crackling in the air, suspended in front of the waiting crowd.

Maybe I accidentally switched to a movie channel by accident.

"Sound on," I say cautiously.

Immediately, the room fills with the sound of people yelling. A caption at the bottom of the screen states that these images are coming from Chicago, and I feel a flicker of concern as I see the strip of lightning dancing in front of the crowd. And then, slowly, I realize I can see figures emerging from the heart of the light.

"It's happening again!" a reporter shouts breathlessly. "It's another portal! There are more people coming through, but it looks different this time! I think they're coming from a different parallel universe!"

I watch as more and more people stream out of the bright light. They look dazed, and there are more and more of them emerging all the time, starting to fill the street. I tell myself that this can't be happening, not again. At the same time, I remember reading some articles that suggested the first portal might not have been an isolated event, that some kind of weakness in space-time could make these events more regular. And as I continue to watch the chaos on the screen, I see a graphic showing that this particular portal is once again running for hundreds of miles across the country. Millions, perhaps billions, of people are coming through from some other world. They're probably copies of people from this world, just like before. Maybe they're fleeing from a war, just like the last group, or maybe they're running from something else entirely. There are so many possibilities.

Suddenly I realize that I'm smiling.

THE OTHER ANN

Also by Amy Cross

The Devil, the Witch and the Whore
(The Deal book 1)

"Leave the forest alone. Whatever's out there, just let it be. Don't make it angry."

When a horrific discovery is made at the edge of town, Sheriff James Kopperud realizes the answers he seeks might be waiting beyond in the vast forest. But everybody in the town of Deal knows that there's something out there in the forest, something that should never be disturbed. A deal was made long ago, a deal that was supposed to keep the town safe. And if he insists on investigating the murder of a local girl, James is going to have to break that deal and head out into the wilderness.

Meanwhile, James has no idea that his estranged daughter Ramsey has returned to town. Ramsey is running from something, and she thinks she can find safety in the vast tunnel system that runs beneath the forest. Before long, however, Ramsey finds herself coming face to face with creatures that hide in the shadows. One of these creatures is known as the devil, and another is known as the witch. They're both waiting for the whore to arrive, but for very different reasons. And soon Ramsey is offered a terrible deal, one that could save or destroy the entire town, and maybe even the world.

Also by Amy Cross

The Soul Auction

"I saw a woman on the beach. I watched her face a demon."

Thirty years after her mother's death, Alice Ashcroft is drawn back to the coastal English town of Curridge. Somebody in Curridge has been reviewing Alice's novels online, and in those reviews there have been tantalizing hints at a hidden truth. A truth that seems to be linked to her dead mother.

"Thirty years ago, there was a soul auction."

Once she reaches Curridge, Alice finds strange things happening all around her. Something attacks her car. A figure watches her on the beach at night. And when she tries to find the person who has been reviewing her books, she makes a horrific discovery.

What really happened to Alice's mother thirty years ago? Who was she talking to, just moments before dropping dead on the beach? What caused a huge rockfall that nearly tore a nearby cliff-face in half? And what sinister presence is lurking in the grounds of the local church?

Also by Amy Cross

Darper Danver: The Complete First Series

Five years ago, three friends went to a remote cabin in the woods and tried to contact the spirit of a long-dead soldier. They thought they could control whatever happened next. They were wrong...

Newly released from prison, Cassie Briggs returns to Fort Powell, determined to get her life back on track. Soon, however, she begins to suspect that an ancient evil still lurks in the nearby cabin. Was the mysterious Darper Danver really destroyed all those years ago, or does her spirit still linger, waiting for a chance to return?

As Cassie and her ex-boyfriend Fisher are finally forced to face the truth about what happened in the cabin, they realize that Darper isn't ready to let go of their lives just yet. Meanwhile, a vengeful woman plots revenge for her brother's murder, and a New York ghost writer arrives in town to uncover the truth. Before long, strange carvings begin to appear around town and blood starts to flow once again.

Also by Amy Cross

The Ghost of Molly Holt

"Molly Holt is dead. There's nothing to fear in this house."

When three teenagers set out to explore an abandoned house in the middle of a forest, they think they've found the location where the infamous Molly Holt video was filmed.

They've found much more than that...

Tim doesn't believe in ghosts, but he has a crush on a girl who does. That's why he ends up taking her out to the house, and it's also why he lets her take his only flashlight. But as they explore the house together, Tim and Becky start to realize that something else might be lurking in the shadows.

Something that, ten years ago, suffered unimaginable pain.

Something that won't rest until a terrible wrong has been put right.

AMY CROSS

Also by Amy Cross

American Coven

He kidnapped three women and held them in his basement. He thought they couldn't fight back. He was wrong...

Snatched from the street near her home, Holly Carter is taken to a rural house and thrown down into a stone basement. She meets two other women who have also been kidnapped, and soon Holly learns about the horrific rituals that take place in the house. Eventually, she's called upstairs to take her place in the ice bath.

As her nightmare continues, however, Holly learns about a mysterious power that exists in the basement, and which the three women might be able to harness. When they finally manage to get through the metal door, however, the women have no idea that their fight for freedom is going to stretch out for more than a decade, or that it will culminate in a final, devastating demonstration of their new-found powers.

Also by Amy Cross

The Ash House

Why would anyone ever return to a haunted house?

For Diane Mercer the answer is simple. She's dying of cancer, and she wants to know once and for all whether ghosts are real.

Heading home with her young son, Diane is determined to find out whether the stories are real. After all, everyone else claimed to see and hear strange things in the house over the years. Everyone except Diane had some kind of experience in the house, or in the little ash house in the yard.

As Diane explores the house where she grew up, however, her son is exploring the yard and the forest. And while his mother might be struggling to come to terms with her own impending death, Daniel Mercer is puzzled by fleeting appearances of a strange little girl who seems drawn to the ash house, and by strange, rasping coughs that he keeps hearing at night.

The Ash House is a horror novel about a woman who desperately wants to know what will happen to her when she dies, and about a boy who uncovers the shocking truth about a young girl's murder.

Also by Amy Cross

Haunted

Twenty years ago, the ghost of a dead little girl drove
Sheriff Michael Blaine to his death.

Now, that same ghost is coming for his daughter.

Returning to the small town where she grew up, Alex
Roberts is determined to live a normal, quiet life. For the
residents of Railham, however, she's an unwelcome
reminder of the town's darkest hour.

Twenty years ago, nine-year-old Mo Garvey was found
brutally murdered in a nearby forest. Everyone thinks
that Alex's father was responsible, but if the killer was
brought to justice, why is the ghost of Mo Garvey still
after revenge?

And how far will the real killer go to protect his secret,
when Alex starts getting closer to the truth?

Haunted is a horror novel about a woman who has to
face her past, about a town that would rather forget, and
about a little girl who refuses to let death stand in her
way.

AMY CROSS

Also by Amy Cross

The Curse of Wetherley House

"If you walk through that door, Evil Mary will get you."

When she agrees to visit a supposedly haunted house with an old friend, Rosie assumes she'll encounter nothing more scary than a few creaks and bumps in the night. Even the legend of Evil Mary doesn't put her off. After all, she knows ghosts aren't real. But when Mary makes her first appearance, Rosie realizes she might already be trapped.

For more than a century, Wetherley House has been cursed. A horrific encounter on a remote road in the late 1800's has already caused a chain of misery and pain for all those who live at the house. Wetherley House was abandoned long ago, after a terrible discovery in the basement, something has remained undetected within its room. And even the local children know that Evil Mary waits in the house for anyone foolish enough to walk through the front door.

Before long, Rosie realizes that her entire life has been defined by the spirit of a woman who died in agony. Can she become the first person to escape Evil Mary, or will she fall victim to the same fate as the house's other occupants?

AMY CROSS

Also by Amy Cross

The Ghosts of Hexley Airport

Ten years ago, more than two hundred people died in a horrific plane crash at Hexley Airport.

Today, some say their ghosts still haunt the terminal building.

When she starts her new job at the airport, working a night shift as part of the security team, Casey assumes the stories about the place can't be true. Even when she has a strange encounter in a deserted part of the departure hall, she's certain that ghosts aren't real.

Soon, however, she's forced to face the truth. Not only is there something haunting the airport's buildings and tarmac, but a sinister force is working behind the scenes to replicate the circumstances of the original accident. And as a snowstorm moves in, Hexley Airport looks set to witness yet another disaster.

AMY CROSS

Also by Amy Cross

The Girl Who Never Came Back

Twenty years ago, Charlotte Abernathy vanished while playing near her family's house. Despite a frantic search, no trace of her was found until a year later, when the little girl turned up on the doorstep with no memory of where she'd been.

Today, Charlotte has put her mysterious ordeal behind her, even though she's never learned where she was during that missing year. However, when her eight-year-old niece vanishes in similar circumstances, a fully-grown Charlotte is forced to make a fresh attempt to uncover the truth.

Originally published in 2013, the fully revised and updated version of *The Girl Who Never Came Back* tells the harrowing story of a woman who thought she could forget her past, and of a little girl caught in the tangled web of a dark family secret.

AMY CROSS

AMY CROSS

BOOKS BY AMY CROSS

For more information, visit:

www. amycross.com

AMY CROSS

27583554R00161

Printed in Great Britain
by Amazon